RESOLVING RUMORS

LOVED FOR THE HOLIDAYS
BOOK THREE

ANNE STORM

with
CHRISTINE MICHELLE

Cover *Art/Photography* licensed via Deposit Photos
Editing: Christy Sears
Proof reading: Beth Diloreto

Paperback Edition
ISBN: 979-8-89706-004-7

For all the drama lovers out there.
This is 10% romance and 90% drama bomb! Enjoy!

TRIGGER WARNINGS

This novel is a relationship in trouble story that includes cheating (even though there is dubious consent as a circumstance). Fair warning: As implied by the dedication, this is a messy story and is more drama than it is romance. While there is a happily ever after, we don't get there until the very end.

Cheating *(in case you missed it before)*
Strong language
Steamy sexual situations
Pregnancy
Questionable paternity
A quickie wedding to the wrong person
Reverse Age Gap (she's seven years older)
Conniving other woman drama
Conniving (supposed) friend drama
Dubious Consent (not between main characters)
Secret romance (because of embarrassment)
Blackmail
And probably some other stuff. This series is not meat for safe readers.

1

VICTORIA

"Why?"

That one stupid word was all I could manage, and even as it left my lips, I knew I wasn't ready to hear the answer just yet. Instead of listening to him, I turned around and left.

"Victoria, wait! Aren't you even going to hear me out?"

"Why should I, Devin?" It hurt too much to turn back around and look at him. All I could see was the scene I'd just walked in on. The one that let me know that my boyfriend's public girl-friend – his beard to keep people from looking too closely at our relationship – wasn't as fake as he'd always led me to believe. His dark hair was mussed like someone had been running their fingers through it, and I couldn't be too sure at that point if it had been him or her.

"Come on, Vic." He sighed. "That's not fair and you know it. It was once and you were out on a date with someone else."

"You've been out on a date with someone else how many times? The difference is that mine was a set up by my mother and I didn't even remotely enjoy it. Yours has been with the fake girl-friend that you swore you weren't sleeping with, but suddenly I walk in on her talking to you about the baby you two are responsible for?" A dark chuckle escaped me. "Tell me which scenario seems fair. I never slept with anyone else and you were apparently fucking your fake girlfriend the whole time."

"It's not like that. If you'd just let me..."

"No. As far as I'm concerned, you made your choice when you stuck your dick in Justice – apparently raw – and got her pregnant. That went a little beyond the whole, 'fake relationship' terms that were set up in the beginning. I'm assuming you two have had your own rules all this time that I knew nothing about."

"You're the one who insisted on the secrecy and you're dead wrong. It was one time, Vic. Once."

"Well, Devin, that's one time too many, especially since you managed to knock your girlfriend up in the process."

"Wife," he huffed the word out reluctantly.

"Excuse me?" The question exploded from me as if painful shards of glass had just ripped me apart from the inside. I didn't want to, but I had to turn back around to see his face as he tried to explain to me how he could have possibly married someone else. Someone who wasn't me.

"When she told me, we ran off and got married because..." I couldn't bear to see him look so wrecked by his admission, as if it pained HIM. The love of my life married another woman. A woman he apparently knocked up at some point while we were dating. If it was possible to die of a broken heart, I might just crumple to the ground on the spot.

"Stop!" My shout bordered on the hysterical. "That's enough."

I was not proud of my actions, but I turned and ran from the only man I'd ever loved. I couldn't do it any longer. I couldn't stand there and face him as the woman he got pregnant, and married behind my back, stood in the background smirking at me.

I'd always thought our situation was ideal because she was involved in a taboo romance with her father's best friend – who happened to be a married man. It meant that she and Devin formed the perfect beard relationship. He helped to conceal her activities, and she kept my little brother, Dallas, off our backs.

I should have known if she didn't have any issues carrying on a clandestine relationship with a married man, especially one so close to her own family, that she would have zero qualms about sleeping with her fake boyfriend – my man. The thing that made it easy to overlook that possibility had been that I had absolute faith in Devin.

I really should have known better. She was age appropriate for him, and didn't come with the baggage that was my brother and the rest of our family. She was also a petite blonde with unnaturally large tits. They were natural, but didn't look as though they fit her otherwise tiny frame. Then there was her faux innocent denim blue eyes that everyone always raved about – including my boyfriend when he played the doting partner at her side.

They were married now and expecting a baby together. They were both 22. I was closing in quickly on 29 and 30 loomed in the not-too-far distance. I'd spent the past three years in a relationship with the man. Well, we spent two years in a secret relationship after a year where Devin chased me until he finally wore me down.

My eyes blurred with unshed tears as I made it to my car, got inside, and flipped the locks before Devin could come after me and grab it open. I had the car turned on before I glanced up and realized he never even bothered to follow me. Instead, he made his way back toward the bitch, who conveniently had her arms wide open for him to step into.

I guess that picture was worth a thousand words and all of them pointed to the fact that I'd been the toy. All along, I'd been the other woman in my own relationship and hadn't realized it. How fucking stupid was I?

2

DEVIN

"I'm so sorry, D."

I stepped into Justice's waiting arms and allowed her to hold me for a minute because I felt like my whole body might fly apart at seeing the damage I'd done to the only woman I ever wanted to marry. Newsflash – it wasn't the wife who was there to hold me when everything fell apart. No, the woman I wanted to build a life with had been too busy keeping me hidden in the shadows. One night of resentment on my part meant everything was over.

"Wow, she just gave me a hateful look," Justice sniped. I glared up at her and took a step back before I glanced back over my shoulder to see Victoria swipe angrily at the tears on her face just before she flew out of the driveway.

"What do you expect?" I growled angrily. "We both made promises to her. Promises that we broke and then compounded by the decisions we made on top of that."

"Well, my promise didn't mean shit, since she doesn't factor into my life."

"She factored into mine. Did that not mean anything? Do I not mean anything to you?"

Justice grinned at me. "Of course you do, husband."

"Don't call me that!" I snapped.

The marriage had been another in a series of complete panic-induced fuckups on my part. We didn't even know if the baby Justice carried was mine or Brody Hinton's. Brody being her 43-year-old married boyfriend. I shook my head free of that mind fuck. Justice had been panicked, too. She begged me to make it look legitimate or else her parents might find out, disown her, and she wouldn't be able to take care of a baby on her own.

How I convinced myself that it was my problem was beyond me. It really wasn't my problem. The chances that I'd impregnated Justice were slim-to-none.

We slept together once, and I didn't even remember the part where I was supposedly inside her – though she swears it happened. I believed her, considering she told me as she apologized for allowing things to go that far while we were both drunk off our asses.

"We are married now," Justice insisted.

It took me a minute to sort my thoughts before I was able to respond. "We need to go back inside and sit down for this conversation."

"Fine." Justice turned on her heel immediately and walked into the house while I meandered in slowly, wondering if the one thing I always dreamed of was now lost to me forever. I'd been in love with Victoria Mercer since the day I met her when I was 12-years-old. My chest cracked wide open thinking that today would be the last time I saw her. That wasn't even the worst case scenario. She was my best friend's big sister, that meant we'd probably see one another again. The problem was, who would she be with when I saw her next? Judging by how everything worked out today it wouldn't be me.

When I finally made my way back into the house, I sat next to Justice and turned so that we were sort of facing one another while still sitting side-by-side. I pulled her hand into mine – the one that now had a ring adorning it that tied her to me. I felt sick to my stomach at the sight and let her hand go to run my fingers through the short hair on my head in frustration. As luck would have it, the ring she placed on my finger snagged on my hair as a reminder of just how fucking off the original plan we had gone.

"You know that I'm in love with Victoria."

Justice shrugged her shoulders and pouted her lips as if it was news to her and it made her unhappy. "It doesn't really matter, considering she wouldn't hear you out!"

I stared at Justice, as if seeing her for the first time. "Are you kidding right now? How would you react if you just found out your boyfriend of two years might have gotten another woman pregnant and married her too?"

"She's the one that agreed to this whole situation to begin with. She had to know it was possible that we would end up hooking up."

"She literally put down rules that we both agreed to, that stated otherwise. Not to mention she thought you were in love with Brody. I imagine that's the only reason she did agree, was that you already had a man you loved."

"Still, you would have to be stupid to throw a younger, better looking woman at your secret boyfriend and not expect things to happen between them." She giggled. "I mean," she tossed her hand back-and-forth between our two bodies, "look at us. We're both gorgeous people. Of course, we were going to fuck at some point. I'm honestly surprised it took you as long as it did."

"I don't even remember ever being naked with you, let alone fucking!" I reminded her. "You are not the woman I want."

Her brow arched higher as I stated that. "Well, I'm the one you knocked up and married."

"Stop. We both know the chances that kid is mine are almost nil."

"We don't know anything yet," She insisted.

"I may have acted out of a knee-jerk reflex when I married you, but only a DNA test will convince me that the baby you're carrying is mine." Her lips puckered like she tasted something sour.

"That doesn't change the fact that we're still married and everyone will know that soon enough."

"An annulment is easy enough to obtain, since we never consummated our vows."

"Or we could consummate our vows and give this a shot," she insisted as her hand trailed up my chest and she attempted to wrap her fingers around my neck.

"Stop!" I shook her off and stood to move across the room. "We're not doing that. What about Brody?"

"He has a wife of his own, in case you've forgotten. I don't know what you want from me. You promised you would be there to help protect me from my situation. Just because your situation blew up in your face doesn't mean you aren't obligated to keep helping me. We are married. I am pregnant. My family still can't know that this baby might not be yours."

"If we tell everyone that it is mine, then it means that I can never fix things with Victoria."

Justice pulled her hair around as if to shield herself behind it and then she shook her head like the thought was easy enough to shake off. "And what will you do if the baby is yours? You'll lose her anyway. No matter what happens between us, there is no way that Victoria will help you raise a baby we made together. Our child will always be a reminder of how she didn't mean that much to you."

"What the fuck is that supposed to mean? She means everything to me!" I argued.

Justice made a noise of disapproval. "Really? Then why in the hell did we get drunk together and end up having sex?"

"I wish I knew."

My unwanted wife rolled her eyes at me. "Oh, you knew exactly what you were doing that night. You might have been thinking about your precious little Victoria, but those thoughts revolved around fucking me to forget she was out with another man that night. It's really convenient how she forgot she was on a date with another man."

"Did you set this up on purpose so that Vic would be here to hear us discussing the baby and marriage?" There was a little niggle at the back of my mind that told me something wasn't right. Justice pushed too hard to get me to accept the end of my relationship with Victoria. I had to change the subject though because just thinking about how Vic went out on a date with some other man still made me feel downright homicidal. I hoped like hell no one ever told me who she was out with.

I was so lost in thought I almost missed the sarcastic sounding giggle that came from Justice. "How was I supposed to know she would show up here today? Besides, maybe you should have been honest with her since the first day we woke up together. At the very least, you should have clued her in the minute I told you I was pregnant, or any time before you married me. Don't try to put this on my shoulders, D. I didn't do anything that you're trying to make me guilty of. You need to accept responsibility just like Victoria does."

"She didn't do anything wrong."

"She has kept you locked in a hidden relationship for two years because she's embarrassed to tell her family that you're together. What part of that isn't wrong? At least in my case, I'm not ashamed of you or anything else. I'm protecting my lover from the fallout of us having a relationship at the wrong time. She's just protecting herself."

Justice wasn't wrong about any of that. I had gone about everything all wrong, starting with Vic's demands to keep our relationship secret. I should have forced the issue long ago. It had been two years since we officially started dating. The minute she said yes to that first date, I should have told her brother. The only reason I hadn't was because she knew it would cause a strain between her and the rest of her family. I had to respect that, but I think we took it all too far and made everything worse. My fake relationship to throw everyone off our trail, and to help Justice out with her situation, made it impossible for her family to take me seriously as her boyfriend if and when we did finally come clean.

Now, with a pregnancy and a marriage in the mix, everything was infinitely messier. Hindsight was a bitch because we should have seen this coming. We should have already factored in how Vic's family would perceive things after we fooled them for so long with my fake relationship to Justice. Our story was never going to have the happy ending I always envisioned, and that was on me for not standing up for our relationship from the very beginning.

3

VICTORIA

"WHAT'S GOING ON WITH YOU?"

I looked up to see that my little sister Katy was standing in the doorway of my bedroom. I'd come home, to my parent's house because I didn't want Devin to go looking for me at my place. If my heart wasn't so broken, I'd laugh that thought off. He hadn't even bothered to chase after me for the length of his driveway. He'd run straight into the arms of his new wife instead. The chances of him going out of his way to search for me anywhere were nil.

"The man I've loved for two years is playing happy families with his new wife and the baby they have on the way," I admitted sulkily before I remembered to hold my tongue.

"Devin is a dipshit."

I spun around so quickly that I damn near gave myself whiplash. "What do you mean, 'Devin'?"

Katy rolled her eyes at me. "Everyone else in this house might have their heads buried in the sand about anything not in their general orbit, but as the youngest Mercer, no one ever really notices me on the fringes watching everyone else.

Houston is a miserable sap who needs to fire that horrible

woman who tried to trap him with a baby that wasn't his," Katy stated about our oldest brother. "Austin is an idiot for stringing Jordan along. He thinks when they hook up that it is free of strings and isn't interfering with their friendship at all. She thinks she'll eventually make him love her in a romantic way. They're both wrong."

If I ever doubted that Katy knew more than any member of our family, I was quickly being schooled in how wrong I'd been. My sweet little sister started in on our youngest brother, then. "Dallas is hiding the biggest secret of all, but I won't give that one away because I can't wait to see everyone's faces when they find out." She gave me a censuring look. "You really shouldn't underestimate him. He pretends to be a fuck up while he's probably the best adjusted of all of us."

"Yeah? What's your secret then, little sister?"

"My secret is that I'm the boring ghost of the family. No one really pays attention to me. So, I keep everyone else's secrets."

"Not very well," I scoffed in response. "You just divulged everyone's secrets to me."

My sister laughed then. "No, those were blatant things anyone who pays attention would notice." Katy winked at me. "That doesn't get you off the hook. Why were you hiding your relationship with Devin for so long, anyway? And why would you put that black widow of a woman in the mix and think that something awful wouldn't happen?"

"She is dating someone."

Katy rolled her eyes. "She's dating a married man." There was no emotion in the words she threw at me. At least, there had been none until my sister rolled her eyes even harder and huffed out the most indignant sigh I'd ever heard aimed at me. "You seriously thought a home wrecker could be trusted with your boyfriend for nearly two years?" My sister shook her head at me. "I might be the youngest, but with the exception of Dallas, I'm beginning to think I'm the smartest."

"I loved him," I admitted. "It didn't matter what *she* was. I trusted Devin."

"Well, I guess I can understand. Honestly, the whole *love* thing seems a bit too messy for me. I use all my older siblings as my case study."

"What about Mom and Dad?"

Her shoulders popped up and down quickly. "They're a fluke. I don't think love like that exists anymore."

"Katy," I whispered, wondering just how and when my baby sister had become so jaded.

"What? Don't tell me you don't feel the same right now. You just had your heart trampled. Your boyfriend married someone else, and I'm guessing he didn't talk to you about it first, or you could have set him straight."

"Set him straight about what?"

"I don't think it's his baby."

"How could you possibly know that? He admitted that they…" I couldn't bring myself to say it. Meanwhile, my sister stood in front of me and rolled her eyes once more.

"I think Justice orchestrated whatever he thinks happened so that she could convince him to do exactly what he did. Men are stupid. They will believe literally everything a woman shoves in their face."

"You think she lied about them sleeping together?"

"What did he tell you about it?"

It was my turn to roll my eyes. "If you think my head, or my heart, was able to hear his excuses when I found out that not only was he married to his fake girlfriend, but they were expecting a baby together, then you're not as smart as you think."

"I guess that's fair," Katy pouted. "I'm sorry your heart hurts."

My little sister came and wrapped her arms around my shoulders while I cried into her mid-section as she stood in front of where I was sitting on my childhood bed. If I was ready to be honest with myself, it was just what I needed, though it hadn't been expected from my youngest sibling. She was still in high school. Katy was right about something else though. She was the most overlooked Mercer sibling.

"Can I ask you something?" I nodded my head against Katy's stomach in answer. Before she said anything else, she took a seat beside me. "If you found out that she lied, like I think she did, would you..." Her sweet voice trailed off. "I mean, you love him, so would you forgive him?"

"I don't know. Part of me feels like it's all my own fault because my need to keep us a secret is the reason she was able to weasel her way in as a 'fake girlfriend' to begin with." I used finger quotes when I said fake girlfriend because I honestly didn't know anymore how fake she had been for Devin. "I thought what we had was real, even though we kept it hidden." I wasn't ready to voice the fact that it didn't matter anyway because Devin had married the witch.

"Why did you keep it secret? You're not that much older than him."

I sighed. "I babysat him once, when he and Dallas were like 12 years old. You don't think that's weird?"

My sister wrinkled her cute little button nose at me. "If you had tried to date him then, I would say it was not just weird but criminal. You were both adults when you started dating, though."

"Still, I don't think anyone else in our family would be so at ease about me being seven years older than Devin. I know Dallas wouldn't be, for sure. He would end up hating me and Devin both. His family would probably swallow some of their millions, right before they attempted to pay me off to get me out of his life."

"That's harsh," Katy huffed.

"Well, Miss All-Seeing, feel free to point out any of the lies you heard."

Katy's shoulders slumped as she leaned forward and put her elbows on her knees and rested her chin on her hands. "I guess you were in a tough position. Still, it's been a long time. Why didn't you come clean when you realized you were in love with him? At that point, you had to know it would be easier to just take the hit, plus if you fell in love with him, he was obviously worth it, right?"

"As today's revelations have proved, you never truly know a person, even if you have been tricked by stupid hormones into believing love conquers all."

Katy threw her arm around me once more and pulled me into a side hug. "I'm sorry things didn't work out better. I hope they turn around for you, though. You were mostly happy with Devin, and I think if it wasn't for the secret keeping, you would have been totally happy and so would he."

"Well, it's a little late to speculate about that now, kid."

"It's never too late."

"Katy?" My mom's voice called out from somewhere downstairs. We both looked at the little alarm clock on the bedside table and groaned.

"It's dinner time. Do you want me to pretend you aren't here? You know if Mom realizes, she'll make you come down."

I slowly stood and pulled my sister up and into another hug. "I'll get cleaned up and come down. Thanks for being awesome, little sis."

Katy smiled brightly before she headed out of my room while I took off for the bathroom to wash the tears and heartbreak from my face.

4

VICTORIA

TWO WEEKS PASSED IN COMPLETE EMOTIONAL TURMOIL FOR ME. Two weeks in which I never saw Devin. There weren't any calls, and though he had been sending texts, I couldn't bring myself to look at them. It felt like an insult to have him simply text, as though what we once had wasn't worth more effort than that. I supposed it wasn't the minute he said, "I do" to another woman. Still, I couldn't get what Katy said out of my head. What if Justice had set this all in motion and there really hadn't been a reason for them to marry?

I shook the thought off, again. The truth was, they were married, and all he bothered to do was send me texts. Even if the baby wasn't his, the chances that they hadn't consummated their marriage and refrained from doing so over the past two weeks were slim to none. He'd already gone there after all, or at least he was in a position intimate enough with her that he thought there was a possibility they could have made a baby together.

"Hey, sexy lady! What's shakin'?"

I glanced up to see my brother's long-time best friend, Jordan standing there in front of me. I must have been zoned out and lost in my thoughts for a while to be taken so off guard by her sudden appearance.

"Wow, you were really lost in thought, huh?" She asked after taking the seat next to me. It was the first time I'd been out in public since finding out about my boyfriend's marriage to another woman. I couldn't sit around my office any longer, though. The mouth-breathing jackass I worked for had been openly salivating over my legs again, making me regret my choice in wardrobe.

"I..." My brain shut off. It refused to allow me to tell people that I was "fine" one more time. That wasn't the truth. In fact it was so far removed from the truth that I began to wonder if the people who asked ever really cared about me at all. Couldn't they see the heartache? I felt like it projected outward from me, ready to incinerate any sign of happiness that passed me by.

"Vic?" Jordan asked as she put her hand on top of mine in a comforting gesture. That was when the dam broke and the waterworks began.

"Shit," Jordan peeled a $20 bill out of her purse and threw it on the table and then she wrapped me up in her arms and pulled me from the restaurant. I had only poked at my lunch, and hadn't taken a single bite, but it was no loss. By the time we got to her apartment, I was all sobbed out.

Jordan drowned a poor washcloth in cold water and handed it to me. "For the swelling."

I gladly accepted it and draped it over my eyes, so I couldn't see the damage all the tears had done to my silk blouse. The wet splotches would dry eventually. Besides, I wasn't going back to work. There was no way I could deal with my slime-ball boss again after breaking down.

"Do you want to talk about it?" Jordan finally asked. I broke down and told her the entire story from the beginning to the sad, pitiful end.

"What is it with you Mercer siblings not knowing how to hold onto a good thing?"

My head snapped up. "Excuse me?"

She waved away my angry retort. "Sorry, that was me projecting my feelings. First, I agree with Katy and Devin, the secret keeping was too much. Now, even if you two get back together, you'll have to keep it a secret even longer because it takes a year in this state to get a divorce, and annulments are only granted in very specific cases."

"How do you know that?"

"A girl I went to high school with had to get an annulment when her parents found out about her wedding. The guy she married didn't realize he needed her parents permission because she was under age. She was 17 at the time and he didn't bother asking for her hand. The parents threatened to charge him with statutory rape until he proved that she used a fake ID that said she was 18."

"Sounds like it was fraudulent anyway, since she used a fake ID to marry him."

Jordan shrugged her shoulders. "They still had to apply for an annulment from the courts. Either way, even if it is possible for them to get the marriage annulled it can take months to get that done. If you two get back together, you'll have to hide that until after the marriage has officially ended or everyone will think you were the other woman who broke a marriage up."

My miserable groan was the only response available. I hadn't put much thought into what would happen if Devin and I reconciled because it didn't seem like something he wanted, considering his lack of effort in trying to explain things to me or work anything out.

"It doesn't really matter. He's obviously happy where he is now."

"I doubt that very seriously. Your sister wasn't the only one who noticed the heated gazes between you two. I almost called you out a couple times, thinking you were trying to step into Devin's relationship with Justice. I wish you had told me sooner. I could have been there for you, so this wasn't something you were doing alone. Plus, someone really needed to give you good advice to keep that scheming woman out of the mix to begin with. Back when we were in school, she was always chasing after Dallas or Devin, hoping to land either of them. When it looked like Dallas wasn't going anywhere in life, she upped her game with Devin. Then, her parents sent her away for the first two years of college until she dropped out and came crawling home. Looks like that was just in time to sink her filthy claws into your man."

"I didn't know any of that. Why didn't he tell me there was history between them?"

"Probably because he is just as blind as Austin is when it comes to taking a hint from a woman."

"What's going on between you and Austin?" I asked to shift the focus off me for a while. Jordan had just dumped a bunch of information in my lap, and I honestly didn't know what to do with any of it. So, I buried it to unpack later when I was alone.

"That stupid bitch from college is back."

"The same home wrecking slut who tried to steal him from you before?"

"That would be her. Things were finally going good for us again. We were back on track and he was even giving me that look. I know in my heart he was going to propose. Then she showed up in his life again thanks to that party planner the guys hired for the bar."

"Wait," I stated, completely taken off guard by what she'd just admitted. "You thought Austin was going to propose to you? As in a marriage proposal?" I had to clarify. "I didn't know you two were seriously dating."

"We've dated on and off since high school."

"I knew you were friends with benefits when it was convenient for both of you, but-"

"That's just what he tells people, so it won't look as bad if someone new turns his eye and he drops me again, like he did with Becs."

"What the hell? Are you serious? First of all, why would you put up with that?" I was appalled by my brother's behavior if that was the case. Jordan had been his best friend for life and she'd become a part of our family. It wasn't right that he continued to string her along in that way. A shameful part of me wondered if I was any better, considering the way I wanted to keep Devin a secret.

"Because I love him," Jordan answered. "I hoped that one day he would love me enough to realize we're meant to be. We were almost there..."

"I should put a foot up his ass!"

"No!" Jordan yelled and stood up. My eyes tracked the movement as she paced across the floor of her living room. "I don't want you to say anything. If he comes back to me, it needs to be because I'm who he wants."

"What if he doesn't?" I asked her, knowing that in some way, I was asking myself the same question.

"Then I guess it wasn't meant to be," she admitted quietly. After a breath or two, she threw her shoulders back and shook that thought off. "No, actually, that just means I need to up my game and fight harder!"

"That's the spirit!" I cheered her on. Jordan had been involved in our family for many years, so I hoped that my brother could pull his head out of his ass and do right by her. Besides, they were already best friends. That meant they could be good together in the long run.

We sat quietly for a bit before I turned to Jordan, who had finally parked her butt beside me on the couch again. "What do you think I should do?"

"It's up to you. If you love him, then you have to fight. Just know that when you do, the secret will still be there, unless you no longer care about what other people think of the two of you together. Considering who you work for, that might be an issue now."

The ball of breathing slime that I worked for was a shark of a divorce attorney. Jordan was right, know matter what, Devin and my previous relationship would have to remain a secret, but so would anything we had going forward until after he managed to get an annulment or divorce. That was if he even wanted to leave Justice. Who knew?

I reached over and grabbed Jordan's hand in mine. "Thank you for unknowingly rescuing me from a depressing lunch."

"You needed to cry it out and talk to someone who would understand, Vic. I'm always here for you. Austin isn't my only friend in your family, you know?"

"I know. Thank you. I'm going to head back home after I call work and explain that I got a nasty case of the shits after eating lunch."

"Ew, why?" Jordan asked as she pulled a face.

"Serves that asshole right for leering at my legs in this skirt all day. Now, he can imagine the shitastrophy that happened during my lunch break instead."

"He might be into that."

"Gross! That's disgusting!"

"So is your boss," she countered.

I nodded and got up to leave, but not before I wrapped my friend in a giant hug. "I hope Austin realizes what a gem he has with you."

"Me too. Maybe Devin will have the same epiphany and we'll both end up with our happily-ever-afters."

I left with a lighter heart than when I'd arrived. Maybe things would work themselves out. The first thing I had to do was go home and read a bunch of text messages to see if the man I loved was worth the fight.

5

VICTORIA

AFTER I GOT HOME, I THREW MY PHONE ON THE CHARGER BY MY bed and left it as I went in search of comfy clothes and a hot shower. Once I washed away all the tears and desperation from earlier, I would shore up enough strength to read through all the messages Devin left for me. It was possible that I waited to read them for no reason. What the hell was I going to do if those messages were about how happy he was with his wife now? It must be refreshing not to have to hide being in a relationship. Besides, Jordan was right. His marriage was another obstacle in ever going public with our relationship.

I let the hot water melt the tension from my shoulders and tried not to think too hard about what awaited me once I got out of the shower. Part of me couldn't stand the thought of never having Devin in my life again. Well, he would still make appearances as my brother's best friend, but how badly would that hurt? Family events he might be invited to would no longer be a place I felt welcome, even if my family didn't understand why. There was no way I could watch him bring his wife and baby around.

The baby.

It was part of the equation I hadn't let myself dwell on yet.

Dwell... I laughed at that. No, I hadn't even given the baby a single thought. The only time the presence of a baby in the mix even entered my mind before now was the brief mention I gave of Justice's pregnancy when I recapped my situation for Katy and Jordan. How had I not considered what things would look like if the baby turned out to be Devin's?

It meant that even if everything worked out and we became a couple, we would have to raise that baby and co-parent with Justice forever. I wasn't sure if that was something I could do. Then again, I hadn't even processed the pain it would cause me to know that Devin had a child with someone else first - while we had been a couple. My heart hurt just thinking about that. More tears leaked from my eyes as it all hit me once again. How in the hell was I supposed to cope with the fact that the love of my life might have made a baby with someone else?

I swiped angrily at my tears as I made my way to the bedroom where my phone taunted me with its presence. Those messages I failed to even look at could say anything. They could be a good-bye, a confirmation of my worst fears, an apology, or...

"Fuck it!" I yelled at myself as I stomped across the room and snatched the damned phone up like it had personally offended me, and I was about to teach it a lesson in manners. I angrily swiped until I got to my texts from Devin, and then I scrolled back to the last one I'd replied to before I showed up at his house unannounced to find out he was married to his pregnant fake girlfriend - err wife.

"Agghh!" I shouted into the room in frustration and then leaped onto my bed to get comfortable for whatever fresh hell and heartache awaited me.

> Devin: I wish you would let me explain! Please, call me back or tell me I can come there, so we can talk in person.

> Devin: Vic, please. We can't leave things like this.

Like what? I wondered. He married another woman. That definitely felt like the end of us, even if he hadn't allowed that to sink in yet.

> Devin: Vic, I love you. We've both had our moments where we were angry and frustrated over our situation. This is no different.

"No different?" I yelled at my phone. "No fucking different? You slept with someone else, you son of a bitch!"

> Devin: That wasn't fair. I know this is different and I am so fucking sorry. It was only that once and I was so fucking drunk I don't even remember doing anything with her beyond commiserating that our real significant others were out with other people that night.

I hadn't gone through with the blind date my mother set up for me. Sure, I met the guy and then… Well, we didn't even make it past the threshold of my apartment before we went our separate ways with me feeling queasy as hell and him obviously disappointed. I still felt bad that he might have taken my rejection as a mark against his looks or something. He had been perfectly acceptable, if only I had actually been single. Not that my mother had known I wasn't single. Again, that was all my fault.

I was hard pressed to figure out why I had demanded we remain in a secret relationship now that things had blown up in our faces so spectacularly. I couldn't even tell my family, outside of Katy, and she was barely an adult. Despite her noticing everything, I didn't want to put the burden of my complicated relationship on her shoulders.

"I think I need a therapist," I whispered into the empty room. Talking to myself had become a habit since I found out my boyfriend married another woman. It was like I couldn't process any of the thoughts that scrambled around in my mind until they were spoken. Speaking some of them was never going to happen though. It made everything real. The whole baby situation being one of those things that I refused to speak aloud. I had to keep thinking that my sister was right and the baby really did belong to Brody, not Devin.

I glanced back down at my phone at the next message.

> Devin: I love you. Whatever you're thinking, whatever horrible shit is playing out in your mind, I need you to remember that I love YOU - Vic. It's always and will only ever be you.

> Devin: Please, talk to me baby. I miss hearing your voice and seeing your smile. Miss lying beside you at night dreaming of our future together.

That last one got me. We couldn't even have a future together because he'd given it away to the woman who was supposed to be his fake girlfriend.

I replied directly to that message.

> Victoria: It's hard to plan a future when your supposed fake girlfriend already stole it out from under me. The baby. The marriage. That was all supposed to be mine and yours together and you took that from us. YOU DID THAT. What did you expect would happen, Devin?

> Devin: It was a mistake. It doesn't have to be this way. We can fix everything and come clean to our families.

> Victoria: So you had your marriage annulled then?"

> Devin: No.

Victoria: So, I'm supposed to come clean to my family that I am the other woman who wants to break up a marriage with a woman you possibly got pregnant? And do you know how long it takes in this state to get a divorce if she doesn't agree to an annulment? Not that it matters since you obviously aren't planning to do that.

Devin: What do you want me to do? I had a knee-jerk reaction to a situation that would have never happened if you hadn't wanted to keep us a secret for so long.

Victoria: Once again, you fucking another woman and marrying her is all my fault.

Devin: I didn't say that.

Victoria: That's exactly what you said. I don't know why I bothered trying to talk to you.

Devin: I resented being a secret. Okay? That was part of the problem and I know, I agreed to it. I agreed to the stupid fake dating. I agreed to everything, but it tore me apart to hear that you were going out on a date with another man. It fucking broke something inside of me and I realized that none of what we were doing was okay. I needed you to be mine 100%. Out in the open. In private. Just mine.

Tears rolled down my cheeks and splashed down on my phone screen as I responded.

Victoria: Funny, but I needed you to be mine too and when I refused to go on a date with someone else because of my feelings, and I planned to tell you that we needed to come clean to everyone, you were busy fucking a baby into another woman.

I threw my phone after I hit send on that last message. It would do no good to keep going round-and-round in circles about everything that had happened to tear us apart. The truth of the matter was that even though I had come to the conclusion that we needed to come clean to our families, I was still racking my brain trying to figure out how to do that while my boyfriend avoided me for a few days. Then, when I finally got the nerve to go have the conversation with him a few weeks later, I found out he married Justice because she was pregnant.

My timing was spectacularly bad, but at least I hadn't embarrassed myself by having that conversation with a man who hadn't come clean to me about sleeping with someone else. Maybe, in the back of my mind, I knew. His whole demeanor had changed toward me in the month or so after that awful date my mother set me up on, even though I had backed out. By the time I worked up the courage to tell Devin it was time to come out into the open with our relationship, he had already moved on and simply hadn't told me yet.

My phone beeped with incoming messages, but I ignored the sound and left my phone where it was on the floor and burrowed deep under my covers. I didn't have the energy to deal with my messy life anymore. Truthfully, I didn't have energy for much of anything. It might have had something to do with the fact that I also couldn't remember the last time I'd eaten, but my money was on every bit of my energy being sapped away by my broken heart.

6

DEVIN

I couldn't believe Victoria. How dare she pretend she was about to tell me she wanted to come clean! I typed out an angry message that I'd probably regret later.

> Devin: That's pretty fucking convenient, considering you waited two years and it just so happens that you decided to come out in the open with our relationship when you had a date.

She didn't answer. I glanced again at the text I had sent after five minutes and it was still only showing as delivered, not read. I sent another one because the first didn't express well enough how I felt about her last text.

> Devin: I don't believe you, Vic. I think you're saying that as an afterthought to make me feel bad for what happened. I already feel like complete shit. There's no need to dump salt on the wound.

I sent that message, and waited for her response, even though I regretted my angry tone. My emotions should have been directed at myself. Logic didn't seem to apply where my feelings were concerned, though. The problem was that my frustrations continually bled over to Victoria instead. I hadn't lied about the building resentment of being in a secret relationship with her. It was fucked up whenever I had to go out on a fake date with Justice and some of my friends would be there loved up with their women. Even Dallas being able to freely pull any single chick into his embrace for the night rankled. I never had that experience with Victoria unless we damn near left the state to have a date night.

Justice would sometimes try to play up public displays of affection when people were watching us, but I always pushed her off or found a way to redirect our focus to someone else. There were times when I had to simply get up and go to the bathroom to catch my breath because she was coming on so hard.

My phone dinged and I snatched it back up expecting to see a message from Victoria fighting with me some more. I was disappointed to see that it was from Jordan. I went to school with her alongside Austin and Dallas, but we were never really good friends. I thought she was a bit too clingy with Austin, but he seemed to enjoy her attention whenever he wasn't dating someone else.

> Jordan: You completely broke Victoria. I spent hours with her today as she sobbed on my shoulder. She told me about how she went to tell you that she was ready to not be a secret anymore and found out you married that skank who has been jonesing to trap you or Dallas into something since high school. I told her all about that, by the way. You should have clued her in to Justice's obsession with you before you let Vic agree to her being your fake girlfriend. I feel like you knew this would happen.

Devin: I have no clue what you're talking about.

Jordan: Oh, please! Everyone knew that Justice only gave up on Dallas because he looked like he was going nowhere and then she set her sights on you. She would have dug her claws in sooner had her family not sent her out of state for college for a couple years. Funny how she managed to show up at the right time when you needed a fake girlfriend to take the heat off your relationship with Victoria, huh? Ever wonder how she managed to wiggle herself into that position?

Devin: Are you fucking serious? She has someone who has to remain a secret too. It wasn't like that at all.

Jordan: You're an idiot if you think her daddy's best friend is who she wanted to get her hooks into. Sure, he has money, but his wife will take half of everything in a divorce and she knows that. Plus, she doesn't want to be a stepmom to his kids who are older than she is. Nope, idiot. You were her mark all along. Congrats on falling dick first into her plan and destroying Victoria in the process.

I stared at that text for the next thirty minutes before I realized Victoria still hadn't messaged me back. I wasn't doing this shit again. There was no way we were going to keep going on the attack with one another followed by the silent treatment for weeks on end. Something had to give and if it had to be me, then so be it.

Fuck that.

It should be me. Vic was right. I was the one that completely fucked the situation and all because I was jealous as fuck that she would be going out on one fucking date with another man while I'd been parading Justice around on dates all over town for more than a year.

That was something else Victoria had been right about. I didn't realize what an emotional toll it probably took on her to see me take Justice out on dates. We went to dinner, usually in groups, and movies sometimes. There was the odd farmer's market run and that art show that Vic really wanted to go to but she ended up there alone while Justice paraded me around the exhibits.

It was only in looking back that I realized Jordan might have had a point. Justice had never been interested in art before. She claimed Brody was supposed to be at the exhibition with his wife and she wanted to make him jealous. We never saw Brody that night, but I did have to watch as Vic left early. She claimed to have a headache when I checked on her via text, but now that I had more perspective and Austin's bratty best friend whispering her secrets in my ear, things didn't look so cut and dry.

"Never should have agreed to any of this," I mumbled as I stuffed my foot into my boot.

"What did you agree to?"

I looked up to see Justice in the doorway. She had her head cocked just so, and once again, she wore barely anything on her body. "What are you doing here?"

"I stopped over to talk to you because my parents are being difficult."

"What does that mean?"

"Well, they know we're married and they don't want me coming back home now. They said I'm your problem now that you married me." It was only then that I noticed the bags at her feet.

"Why are your bags outside my bedroom door?" Justice had been staying in my guest room most nights for the past couple weeks, but I had never agreed to her officially moving in. Even if I had, she should know better than to bring her stuff to my side of the house. The house I owned was a two bedroom, two bath but it was split down the middle. The living room and kitchen were at the center and then there was a master suite on either side. There was absolutely no reason for her to bring her bags to this side.

"Well, you and Victoria are over." Justice rolled her eyes when she said that, like it was a given. Then she patted her slightly rounded tummy and grinned. "We're having a baby and we're married. What will people think when they come over and we're living in two separate rooms? Besides, we need to turn the other room into a nursery."

"What the fuck?" I yelled at her without thinking. Her big blue eyes blinked a couple times as her pink lips parted in shock. "We are married in name only, and that's going to change very soon. That baby," I pointed at her belly, "most likely isn't mine, especially since you wouldn't be showing already if it was." Her eyes narrowed down into thin slits that would spit venom at me if possible. "And Vic and I are not over. We're in the middle of a rough patch, but we are not over. We never will be."

Justice scoffed out a half-hearted laugh. "You're delusional. She will never take you back after you slept with me. Add in the fact that you married me too, and Victoria will never forgive you. You might as well give up on her because that ship sailed the minute you agreed to me being your fake girlfriend. The two of you just didn't know it yet."

I could see the victory sparkle in her eyes. She thought she won me right out from under my real girlfriend. Jordan's texts came back to mind. "Did you ever truly have a thing with Brody, or was that some elaborate lie to hook me into a fake relationship until you could make it real?"

"Brody and I fuck from time-to-time but it was never going to be anything more than that. He won't leave that stupid cow he's married to because she'll take him for everything. Besides, I've always had my eye on you, and let's face it, you're younger and have more potential with less baggage at this point in your life."

"Unfuckingbelievable." Every syllable was growled out together as a singular word that emphasized my growing frustration. Jordan had been right. This was all some ruse to get me on the hook, and all it took to get me onboard was for Vic's mom to set her up on a blind date - a date she apparently never even went on.

I stared into Justice's Navy blue eyes and noticed the way they pulled a little tighter at the corners as she tried to hide a wince. "Is that baby even mine?" Her hesitation should have told me everything I needed to know, but it could also simply mean that she didn't know.

"Anything is possible."

"Really? That's what you're going with?"

She nodded and then turned her back on me. "There's no way to know until after I give birth, so strap in and prepare yourself to be the best husband ever for the next few months." She flounced back out of the room as if my whole world being shattered at my feet didn't fucking matter.

All I could think was that she had truly done it on purpose. After hearing what Jordan had to say about everything, it made me wonder if I had been Justice's target from the very beginning. What if she never gave a rat's ass about Brody?

"We played right into her game," I whispered to myself.

7

VICTORIA

THE FEELING THAT SOMETHING WASN'T RIGHT PLAGUED ME UNTIL my sweet dream of a happily ever after with Devin poofed out of existence as my awareness of the real world came back online. A quick sniff of the air confirmed my original thoughts upon waking. It smelled like breakfast in my house. The savory aroma of seasoned hash-browns and bacon frying forced my mouth to produce an overabundance of saliva before my brain bothered to ask the all-important question. "Who in the hell is cooking breakfast in my house?"

My eyes darted to the bedside table where my phone still sat face up, quiet as a church mouse. After I reached for it, I quickly discovered the last text or call I received was from Devin the day before. For a moment, I debated calling 9-1-1, but what were the odds that a criminal broke in and stuck around to make breakfast?

Slowly, I got up and put on a robe, secured it tightly enough that it wouldn't come loose and show off the too-thin tank top and panties I'd worn to bed the night before. I scooped my long blonde tresses up and wound them into a messy bun before I made my way out of the bedroom. I'd read somewhere that long hair, especially a ponytail, was your worst enemy when attacked. If it was effective to roll my eyes at myself I would. I'd already determined that whoever broke into my house to make breakfast must be friendly.

At least, I hoped so.

When I rounded the corner, I was greeted with a sight that instantly made my heart leap with joy and grieve all at once. How in the hell was that even possible?

Devin stood there in front of my stove, shimmying to soft music he had playing from his phone as he scrambled up some eggs to go with the hash-browns and bacon he cooked up. He always bemoaned that he broke the omelets every time and I showed him that a good scramble, while not as pretty as an omelet, could have the same damn ingredients in it.

His ass was well defined in the jeans he wore while the t-shirt hugged his upper body in a way that showcased just how much he must have been working out lately. He was thicker, more muscular than he had been just a month ago. I guess marriage looked good on him.

It made me sick to my stomach to think about. My gaze shifted to the floor where I glared at it for not opening a hole there to swallow me up. If ever there was a time to disappear into the abyss, it was when you realized your ex was doing far better after he replaced you with another woman.

"Hey, I meant to surprise you with breakfast in bed." I glanced up to see that Devin moved around the counter and was headed toward me.

"Why?"

"Why what?"

"Why are you here, Dev? Shouldn't you be at home serving up food to your pregnant wife instead of me?"

His sigh nearly sent me into a homicidal rage. My brewing anger must have shown on my face because he threw his hands up in the air and took a conscious step backward. "We need to talk."

"I think you said everything that needed to be hashed out between us when you said, 'I do' to another woman."

Devin shook his head and for some stupid reason, I couldn't look away from the sadness that iced over his normally warm, caramel hued eyes. It was only then that I noted the dark circles beneath them as well. Maybe I had been too quick to judge his growing physique because the rest of him looked as exhausted as I felt.

"Please, Vic." It was my turn to sigh, though not as dramatically as he had done moments ago.

"Fine. We can talk. At the table though. No offense, but I can't stomach the thought of you in my bedroom anymore."

"Fucking hell, woman." Devin turned back to plate our food as I walked off to the dining table not sure what to do with the jumbled thoughts and questions that clogged up my brain. What were we supposed to talk about at this point? Was there anything that could be said to fix things? I doubted that, but I still deserved better than: "I was jealous of your date" as a reason to throw our whole relationship down the tubes for someone else.

I sat at the head of the table, so that even if Devin tried to sit by my side, he would still be a little further away than if we sat directly beside one another as we used to do. Maybe it was petty of me, but in all honesty, it was more about keeping my distance to preserve my sanity. My heart could only take so much closeness to Devin. I still loved him even as I hated what he'd done to us. I also understood that while he was the one who made the decisions he did that put the final nails in the coffin, it was my desire to keep us a secret that built the damn thing to begin with.

"Here," Devin stated as he pushed a full plate, with silverware on it, in front of me. He set his down on the table and then ran back to the kitchen. When he got back, he had coffee for both of us. He took the seat to my left and pulled his chair as close to the end of the table as was possible without sliding around and practically sitting in my lap.

I took a tentative bite of the western scramble he made. My stomach wasn't exactly up for it, despite the audible grumbles it started to make the minute I smelled breakfast cooking while I was still in bed. While my mind tried to process the fact that Devin was there, in my house, and made me breakfast, the rest of me was still stuck in a weird stage of grief for the relationship we once had. Logically, I knew he wasn't dead, but our breakup felt like something permanent.

"I'm sorry."

"You've said that and it changes nothing." I glanced up into those confused brown eyes of his and laid my fork back down on my plate. "I understand that you are apologetic, maybe even regretful, but it doesn't change anything about the situation. You married another woman. Even if she is pregnant with your baby, and I thought it was possible to forgive you, there is no getting around a marriage."

"There is when it doesn't mean the same thing as it does for everyone else."

I reached forward and grabbed his left hand to hold up between us. "In case you forgot, you married someone else. Not only are you married to Justice, but you seem awfully proud of the fact, considering you're wearing a ring that symbolizes your union to her. If it was all smoke and mirrors, you wouldn't have that on your fucking finger." I pointed at the circle of metal that my eyes had been drawn to repeatedly since I realized he was in my house.

He reached over, took the ring off, and threw it somewhere across the room. "That shit doesn't mean anything to me. She doesn't mean anything. I doubt it is even my fucking baby."

"There was a chance that it was your baby, though, since you married her so quickly." The accusation left me on a whisper, but he still heard it.

"All I know is that I was pissed you were on a date with someone else. I got tore the fuck up drunk and she was there getting wasted right along with me." He sighed so deeply that I could feel the weight of his regret before he spoke again. "When I woke up, we were in bed together and I honestly don't remember how I got there or what happened that night. I was so blitzed." Those last words came out sounding almost like a plea for me to understand.

"When I woke up and saw her naked in bed with me, I threw up." Devin admitted. I kind of knew the feeling because I wanted to throw up after hearing that too.

"What was she doing at your house that night?"

"She knew you had a date and apparently Brody was out for a guy's night with her dad, who bragged to her about them going to see some strip show."

I cringed. "That's just too much yuck to even process."

He nodded. "That's why we were drinking and commiserating."

"You do realize that you go out on dates with the woman you ended up married to all the time, right?"

"That was different. You didn't have to worry..." His voice trailed off when he realized how stupid that sounded.

I huffed out a frustrated noise. "Nothing to worry about there. It's not like you knocked her up, or at least slept naked with her, and then married her without even being good enough to warn me beforehand. Instead, I had to hear about it after the fact, when I came to your house unannounced. And still, it wasn't because you managed to tell me about it. I busted you talking about your sweet little family with your brand new wife. Sure, I can see where that was totally different."

"Fuck!" Devin yelled as he turned his back on me.

"I get that I have some share in the blame for how this happened, because I never should have trusted a home wrecker in a million years."

"She's not a home wrecker." The fact that he jumped to her defense, and so quickly, pissed me off.

"Right, because she's not carrying a married man's baby, and she didn't marry *my* boyfriend behind my back after sleeping with him. No, she doesn't meet the definition of home wrecker at all." Sarcasm laced every word I spoke. "The truth will come out eventually, about whose baby that is, and people are going to be hurt. **She doesn't care!**" I yelled the last bit at him before I moved past Devin to grab some tissue from the bathroom. When I came back out he stared at me, as if waiting for the rest of whatever I'd been saying. So, I gave it to him.

"She smiled at me when she welcomed you into her waiting arms as I took off that day. And you went willingly. Why wouldn't you? You were already *her* husband and wearing *her* ring by then!"

"She's my wife," he whispered.

"Funny, just a few minutes ago, you said none of that meant anything."

He hung his head then. "I feel like I'm stuck between a rock and a hard place here, Vic. I already married her. She's pregnant. Whether its my kid or not, I can't really do anything to upset her at the moment because it might cause issues."

"Well, isn't that convenient. She gets to play happy family with you for the entirety of her pregnancy, and then it will be her postpartum, sleep deprived state that keeps you on the hook. Before long, you'll fall in love with her baby and she'll realize that her real baby daddy isn't going to leave his wife or tell his best friend what a fucking creep he is. I thought it was bad that we were seven years apart, but that man is literally her godfather. He was there to help change her diapers and now she's having his kid."

We sat there in silence for a while as everything I'd just spewed out hung between us like a mile-high wall we couldn't possibly get over.

"Do you think anyone who found out about me seeing you, while you are still married to Justice, would see it is a healthy relationship?"

"Why are you still so damned worried about what everyone else thinks?"

"You mean besides the fact that if people found out I was running around with a married man, while his wife was pregnant, I would lose my job because of the damage it would do to the firm?" I asked.

"Fuck," Devin hissed out as he sat back in his chair and stared at the plate of food that remained mostly untouched in front of me. "I think she set me up. Does that count for anything?"

I shook my head slowly. "Jordan gave me the same impression when we talked, but even if she set it up, you still fell for her trap and now we're all an ocean deep inside the consequences."

"We were already dating in secret. Why can't we continue to do that until I can convince Justice to sign annulment papers?"

"Do you think she'll sign without giving you trouble?"

My heart broke as he shook his head and then hid his face behind his hands as he tried to somehow scrub away all the frustrating truths that made it impossible for us to be together.

"I can't lose you, Vic."

"No, you threw me away without even allowing me any consideration in the choices you made."

"I swear to you, I did no such thing. She hit me with the pregnancy out of nowhere and how her parents were going to disown her, especially if they found out Brody was one of the potential baby daddies."

"So, the only option you two had was to get married? You said before that the chances of the baby being yours was slim. Why not let her take her chances with Brody?"

"And if it turned out to be my kid? You really want me to explain to my kid one day how I hoped they didn't exist and I failed to help their mom?"

"You know that's not what I meant," I argued.

"I get it, but you have to understand, Vic. If that is my kid, then I need to do whatever it takes to make sure he or she is okay."

"You could have moved her in if you were worried, marriage was an unnecessary step and one too far for me to be able to move past."

"You're right about half of that. If I had given myself time to think clearly, I would have seen that too. We can move past this, though. I have to believe that."

I picked up my fork and poked at the breakfast that had grown cold on my plate. "I don't know where that leaves us. The simple fact that it is possible she might be carrying your baby is..." I couldn't even finish the sentence without choking up. "It's fucking heartbreaking, Devin. You chased me. You made me fall in love with you. Then you pulled it all out from underneath me. I took a minute to pull myself together again before I continued. "You did that just when I was finally comfortable enough to say, 'Let's do this publicly,' and that isn't possible now."

"I'm sorry, Vic. We can figure this out, if you'll just give me time to-"

"Why?"

"Why what?" He asked as his eyes hooded over with worry.

"Why couldn't you trust me the same way I put my faith in you for over two years, a year and a half where Justice was in the picture?"

"I don't understand," my former boyfriend said as he took hold of my hand.

"I trusted you on dates with her, in public, and even when you were in private spaces. I put my faith in YOU that we were too important for you to go there with someone else. Why couldn't you do the same for me?"

Devin sighed and squeezed my hand once more. "I was afraid

that you would see how good it is to be out with someone without having to hide from everyone."

"Is that how you felt every time you were on a supposed fake date with Justice?" My stomach hurt from asking the question, so in all honesty, I wasn't sure I could handle hearing his response. He gave it nonetheless.

"No. No, Vic. Not at all. I swear to you, every time I was out with her, all I wanted was for it to be you by my side. Dating her was like having a second job. I was an unpaid actor in this crazy farce and being out with her was nothing more than having to put on a performance."

"Then why would you think it would be any different for me?"

"I don't know. Justice was part of the problem. She came over and talked about how Brody was the love of her life and he was out with his wife and that their dynamic reminded her of us. She insisted that Brody would leave his wife for her one day and that the same thing would end up happening in our situation, only it would be one of us leaving the other because we were tired of having to live in the shadows."

We both sat very still in the light of that assessment. Then Devin spoke again and made me want to crawl under the table and hide away in shame. "It hit me hard because I had been feeling like the other man in an affair, waiting for the day the married woman would finally throw her husband away for me like she promised. There wasn't another man - not yet. When your mom set you up on that date, it was all I could think of. I had been a dirty secret for so long, why wouldn't you choose an easier, more age-appropriate option over me?"

"I need you to know that I never blamed you for everything. I blamed myself for most of what went wrong, because I wanted the secrecy."

He nodded as if he already knew that, and I suppose, on some level, he did. "I don't see how we can make it work now though." I glanced down at his left hand - the one that only a little while ago bore the evidence of his current married status. "For someone who claims he wants an annulment, you were still wearing the ring, as if it was the proud symbol of commitment it is supposed to be when two people get married."

"Fucking hell!" He pointed off into the other room where he had been standing when he threw it earlier. "I already took it off. It means absolutely nothing to me. She means nothing to me. I came here to talk this out because Jordan contacted me and after our conversation, I realized she might be on the right track. I wanted to make a plan with you. A plan to get me out of this mess with Justice and another to get us back together where we belong." Devin huffed and stood as he yanked me out of my chair. "Only this time, we'll be out in the open with everything because I'm not hiding my love for you any longer."

I nodded my head in agreement, like an idiot, before his lips crashed down on mine and sealed his words between the two of us as if it was a sacred vow.

8

DEVIN

IT FELT SO RIGHT TO HAVE MY WOMAN BACK IN MY ARMS, EVEN IF IT was short-lived.

"I love you, Vic. Never stopped. Never will. You are meant to be mine until the end of time."

She rolled her eyes and sniffled all at the same time. I pushed my girl's blonde hair back behind her ears because there was no way I'd be able to secure it in that bird's nest of a bun she had it in before our kiss, and my roaming fingers, fucked it all to hell.

Victoria's lips were swollen from our kiss when I pulled us away from the now cold and ruined shambles of breakfast and into the living room, so we could sit beside one another and hash things out in a healthy and productive way. We had both done enough of slinging accusations and trying to place blame on one another's shoulders. It did nothing but push us further apart and I was done with that.

"What are we going to do about the..." Vic swallowed as if she were choking on the word she refused to say. I positioned us, so that we were both turned inward, facing one another with our knees touching and our hands clasped together.

"I am almost one hundred percent sure that the baby is not mine."

"How can you say that?"

"First of all, because unless she is bloating every time she eats, Justice is already showing."

Vic scrunched her nose up at me. "That should be impossible this early."

"Exactly. Besides, she's the one who claims that we were together sexually, and I have no memory of that." Vic cringed and tried to pull away, but I held strong to her hands. "No, don't push us backward again. I know it isn't easy, but we need to discuss this. I do not remember having sex with, or even kissing, Justice." I let go of one of her hands long enough to tap the side of my head. "Up here is a blank. No memories, I swear it, Vic." When I let go of her hand, it felt like a fucking victory that she placed it on top of our other two that were still wrapped around one another.

"The fact that she was there that night, and Brody was conveniently out to a strip club with her father, is still worrisome. I know her father supposedly mentioned them going out, but she could have made that up, just like she probably made up some of the dates Brody supposedly took his wife on. I believe it was pure coincidence about as much as I believe she's pregnant with my baby."

"You think she went there with the intent to set it up to look like you might have fathered her baby?"

"She fed me enough drinks after she arrived, that she couldn't have been priming me for sex - not in a real way - because the chances of me passing out with that much liquor in my system were far greater than my ability to get hard with a woman who wasn't you."

"Come on, she's a beautiful girl."

"Yeah, objectively, she is. And you know what? She's never made me hard because she's not my type. She's a brat who has no qualms about cheating on or with people. That isn't the type of woman who revs my engine. If it wasn't for our arrangement, I wouldn't even be friends with her because she has no concept of loyalty."

Victoria groaned. "Why did we do this to ourselves? I should have never suggested hiding our relationship, and you should have never agreed to go along with it."

"We're not looking back anymore, baby. We can't change the past. Well, we can't change the parts that count. We can make a plan to move forward and get out from under the bullshit with Justice. Let's work on that, and then we'll work on us, and where we want to be a year from now."

"What if we discover we aren't good for one another?"

"I don't believe that any more than you do. Our problem was never 'us', it was your concern over what everyone else would think about us. I refuse to allow other people's opinions to factor into my happiness because it isn't working. If you decide that you can't be with me because everything has become too messy, then I will have to deal with your decision. For the record, I want you. I don't just want you, Vic, I need you in my life like the air I breathe."

"What if…" She looked away and bit down on her lip, as if she refused to say the one thing that would make or break us. It didn't take a genius to figure out that Vic was worried Justice's baby was mine and what that would mean for us.

"Let's come up with a plan and leave that bit for later when we can get a definitive answer, okay?"

Victoria nodded her head and then quickly switched to shaking it. "I don't think I could…" She hesitated again and I wanted to kick myself in the nuts for ever making her feel this way. Not to mention, the fear I lived with that for some crazy reason the baby turned out to be mine, it would mean that I would lose my woman. The only woman I'd ever loved. There would be no doubt about it. Vic wouldn't be able to handle me having a child with someone else, but she also wouldn't tolerate me abandoning my own kid to be with her. Not that I would ever do that, no matter how much I loved Vic.

"How are we supposed to do this, Dev?" She asked me and the only answer I had was to pull her closer. She snuggled into me as I wrapped my arms all the way around her body and refused to let go.

"We take things one day at a time. Make time for one another. Be honest. Mostly, we plan for the future and work on getting past all the hurts we've caused one another."

"We'll still be a secret."

"Only for a little while longer. I'm working on untangling the mess I made with Justice." I kissed the top of Vic's head and she squeezed me tighter. "As soon as we have a good handle on when that will resolve, we're going to tell our families the truth about everything."

"Well, maybe we can leave some of it out," Vic mumbled into my chest.

"I think it's for the best if they know the full extent, so there are no surprises." I explained.

"Then I hope you're ready for my brothers, and what they're going to do to you, since you cheated on their big sister."

I sighed. "Believe me, baby, I've already come to terms with the fact that my nose will probably never look the same again." Vic's body shook against mine as she laughed.

"Promise me something?" She asked before her beautiful eyes opened up and her head tilted back, so she could look me in the eye.

"Anything."

"No more guesswork."

"What does that mean?" I asked, not understanding.

"It means neither one of us is going to assume things and let our jealousy cloud our judgement. We talk it out or we walk away. I can't go through this again, Dev. It nearly killed me to lose you once. I can't do it again."

I nodded and kissed her before she could say another word. We were on the same page with the communication issues. If we had talked more, about the important stuff, we might not have ever been put in the position to lose one another. There certainly wouldn't have been room for another person to come between us. Knowing that Vic was just as affected by our short split was a double edged sword. On one hand, it was good to know she cared so much. On the other hand, I hated that my actions were the catalyst to her pain. Our pain.

All that was left was to deal with Justice and fix the cracks in the foundation of our relationship that Vic and I had allowed to grow. Once everything was smoothed over, I believed we would finally end up happy together. The only worry I had was how my best friend would take the news, especially since I hadn't been faithful to Vic the first time around. I scrunched my face as I thought the last bit because it rang false in my own mind. Lacking the memory didn't mean I was completely innocent, but it made it impossible for me to agree that I cheated on my girl.

9

VICTORIA

"I DON'T LIKE THAT WE STILL HAVE TO KEEP THINGS SECRET FOR now," I admitted as Devin snuggled me into his body on my couch.

"I know, baby. It won't be for long this time. We're both on the same page about things now and all I need to do is find a way to compel a DNA test from Justice to set this right."

"I heard they could be done during pregnancy, but how accurate is it?"

Devin shrugged and then tightened his hold on me. "Not sure, but the DNA test might not even be necessary if her due date doesn't line up with when she claims we were together."

A shiver ran up my spine. "I hate that you don't know what happened while you were alone with her. My imagination goes to all the places I hope you didn't, but it seems like we'll never know the truth." I always felt sick when I thought about them together, but knowing how he had been so adamant that he didn't remember it happening made it a little worse.

"If you don't remember, and it turns out that you did in fact have sex with her, then it's possible that it was rape. You realize that, right? If you were so inebriated that you can't remember, there's no way you could have consented."

"Not talking about that right now."

"Devin, we have to…"

"No! I'm not going to think about that being possible. It's bad enough knowing you weren't the last woman I was naked in a bed with. I don't want to imagine that she also took advantage of me like that because it would mean you also weren't the last woman I had sex with and that is not acceptable to me."

"You married her because you believed she was the last woman you had sex with."

"I can't explain it to you and make it make sense. Something happened between Justice and me. I am sure about that, but I don't want to… I can't think about it." I felt the hitch of his harsh intake of breath and it rattled me on the inside. There was something he wasn't telling me about that situation, and I didn't think it was because he wanted to keep me in the dark. It was more like he needed to keep himself there.

"There was evidence that we'd been together, Vic. I don't want to tell you more than that because I don't want to hurt you with the details." He didn't have to, since I'd already imagined the worst. "And it is true that I don't remember, but I was so angry about the secrecy, about having to give my time and attention to another woman, about you being with another man. Yes, I was drinking. No, I don't remember, but that doesn't absolve me of cheating on you. It happened. I was angry and jealous enough that it is possible I allowed it to happen. Maybe I hoped that it would cure me of wanting you so much." He shrugged and I moved back so that I could see him fully.

What he was saying broke my heart all over again in a way that finding out about the situation hadn't done before. It broke me because my need for secrecy caused this. It broke me because he got to a point in our relationship where he was willing to throw it away. Mostly, it turned me inside out because he believed what happened was cheating and not that vapid bitch taking advantage of a completely fucked up situation.

"The marriage part was a panic response to finding out I might have cheated on you and gotten her pregnant as a result. The logistics of that being possible didn't even set in until much, much later, Vic. One truth hung in the air the minute Justice told me she was pregnant."

"What was that?" I asked, though I honestly wasn't sure I could handle anymore truths.

"I knew if it was true, and I got another woman pregnant, that you would never forgive me and we would be over. That was what made me go through with it before I could even wrap my head around the fact that Brody stood a bigger chance of being the father. Hell, I didn't even question if she was really pregnant. She showed me an ultrasound photo, but that could have been from anywhere. I was in a panic and thought I lost you completely at that point."

"I hate this." I hated it more because he didn't feel he could come to me before acting on impulse about the impossible situation of having to remain a secret even longer, even if he was right about Justice lying to him about the baby being his.

"You and me both. So, let's do something different. Can I kiss you again, baby? I need to know your lips are mine again."

"Do you?" I teased and turned in his embrace. He wasn't the only one who needed that reassurance. Maybe I was a fool for thinking we could get past everything. Maybe it would all fall apart again tomorrow. The truth was, I missed Devin. I missed the way I felt complete when we were together.

"I do," he answered and those two words sent another shiver of apprehension down my spine, but I tucked them to the back of my mind as his lips met mine. I leaned back as my love moved forward and didn't stop until my back was on the couch and he hovered over me. Our lips met and fused together as our tongues tangled. The tug on my heart wasn't something I could think about though, because everything felt too precarious just yet.

"I love you," Devin whispered as he pulled back from our kiss. His eyes took in everything as he scanned my face and used the fingers that cradled my cheeks to swipe away a rogue tear that fell. "I love you so much, Vic. I can't imagine my life without you in it."

"I love you too, Devin. I don't know how in the hell we're going to get past this, but we need to try." I didn't tell him that there was no way I could continue to live with the misery of our separation. I also didn't tell him that having to keep us a secret any longer would hurt me too. There was no getting around the secrecy until he found out for sure if that baby was his.

"Take me to bed, please," I whispered. Part of me didn't want to go there. The other part of me needed it more than my next breath and there was no logic or reason involved. My heart demanded to be close to him while my head worried about the damage it would cause if...

"Are you sure, baby?"

His voice anchored me in the now instead of the 'what ifs' that plagued our future. My answer was a simple nod of my head before Devin picked me up off the couch and carried me to my bedroom. Maybe it was a mistake, but there was a part of my heart, or maybe it was my soul, that craved his presence.

His touch.

The closeness we once shared.

"Last chance, are you sure?" The man I couldn't stop loving asked me as he gently laid my body on the still unmade bed.

"Condoms?" I asked. It wasn't something we bothered with over the past year of our relationship because we were monogamous and I had an IUD. I could see that the light of excitement diminished from his eyes a bit with my question.

"I was tested after..." I had been too, from the moment I found out they had slept together. "It was only that one time."

"I..." How in the hell was I supposed to tell him that I no longer trusted his word, despite the fact that I wanted to?

"Do you still have that box in the bathroom cabinet?" I tipped my head up once and he left me there to go to the bathroom. When he came back, he brought the entire box with him.

"Are they expired?" It had been a long time since we'd bought that box and then quickly decided we didn't want to bother with condoms any longer.

Devin shook his head. "They're still good." His eyes moved from the box in his hand to meet my nervous stare. "We don't have to, Vic. If you changed your mind or you're worried..." He swallowed thickly as his eyes drifted back to the box in his hand.

"I want this, with us. I guess I just realized that there are lingering trust issues we need to work through."

"Maybe we should wait on this part until we figure that out."

I shook my head. "It's probably the smart thing, but I can't stand the thought that she was the last person you were with either. You are mine. You were supposed to always be mine. If we're doing this, then we need to start by reclaiming what is supposed to be between us." I waved a hand back and forth. "The intimacy we lost, the trust, all of it. We need to... I need to..." I didn't know how to finish that thought, but Devin did. He dumped a few of the condoms from the box down beside me and then leaned in to steal a kiss from my lips again.

"I know, baby. You don't have to find the words because they live in here too." He whispered as he took my hand and tapped it on his chest, over his heart. "You're the piece I've been missing in here, the one that wouldn't let this thing beat properly. I need you just as much."

"Dev..." I whispered, but the rest of his name was lost to another stolen kiss. My free hand wound up and around his neck to hold him close to me. It felt like any minute I would wake up from this dream only to discover that he had never been here making breakfast in my kitchen this morning.

"You've been my dream girl since I was 12, baby. Not letting you go now that I have you."

"I need you inside me," I urged. "Please." I don't remember ever begging Devin before, but it switched him into high gear as he lifted off me and started to remove his clothes.

"Get that robe and whatever you have underneath it off, Vic." His demand was laced with carnal heat that I responded to immediately. I moved into action without giving much thought to the fact that he'd given me a direct order. I unknotted the robe, and slid it from my body, though it remained trapped beneath me. Then I lifted my bottom and pulled my panties down my legs. Just as I moved my arms to lift the tank top over my head, Devin's hands came down on top of mine.

"No, I want to unwrap the final part of my present, baby." He murmured the words as his fingers traced under the tank top and over my belly so slowly that it felt like the best kind of torture. With each inch of exposed skin, Devin's eyes grew heavier and darker. When my breasts were finally exposed, he gave up the slow seduction and attacked my left nipple with his mouth while his hand caressed my other breast and pinched that nipple. My tank top was left to linger around my neck and while it was slightly uncomfortable I couldn't bring myself to finish removing it because my own hands were too busy exploring Devin's shoulders and then his biceps.

"You're bigger," I mused, though my thought ended up spoken aloud.

"Nothing to do but work and work out when you refused to speak to me." He moved up and kissed my lips before he pulled my tank top the rest of the way off my body and tossed it to the floor.

"It's different. You feel like a different person." My admission startled him as his eyes swept back up to meet my own.

"Is that a bad thing?"

"No. I guess it just took me by surprise. We weren't apart that long, despite it feeling like an eternity. Still, you changed in that time and I guess it's messing with my head a bit."

"Turn it off, baby. Let it all go and just be in the moment with me." The last thing he said was another demand before he leaned in and nipped my earlobe. Then he explored my neck while leaving open mouthed kisses all along the column of my throat and down across my collar bone. "You with me now?"

I nodded, but he must not have seen. His tongue swiped across one nipple, then the other before his eyes came up to meet mine again. "You with me?"

"Always," I whispered in response. The smile he gave back made butterflies dance in my stomach. He was a gorgeous man, but even more so when he smiled at me like that.

"Good, then I want you to stay right there while I worship your body. If you can't handle that, I'll tie your ass to this bed until I'm done reacquainting myself with every inch of you."

I shivered despite his threat being hot as hell. Devin noticed and chuckled. "You like that idea, don't you pretty girl?"

"Yes, I think I do."

"Noted. For now," he leaned in and kissed me in the center of my chest and then planted another kiss a little lower and then another lower still. I glanced down as Devin groaned into my lower belly. "Missed the way you taste, smell, and move beneath me." He ran his nose along my abdomen and down further between my legs. "Victoria's sweet honey flavor. I would pay to have it bottled for me if I didn't enjoy getting it directly from the source so much."

I giggled. "You're an idiot," I managed to get out through my laughter.

He shook his head and swiped up my sex with his tongue. "Nope. I'm a lovesick fool. There's a difference."

I'd like to say I thought about all the things that were more important than having sex with my boyfriend - ex boyfriend - maybe on-again boyfriend, but beyond not knowing what we were to one another anymore, I couldn't really think because Devin's mouth descended on me and worked magic on my body.

I hadn't realized how much I had missed the way he worked me over with his mouth, but then he added his hands to the mix and pumped two fingers into me. When he curled them to hit my spot while he nibbled and sucked my clit, I lost my damn mind and screamed out for him to never stop.

"I'd spend forever feasting on you, if you'd let me." His promise came just before he leaned in and joined our mouths, so I could taste myself on his lips and his tongue. Devin slid his cock deep inside me as he did this. I had a moment of panic when I realized how quickly he made it up to my mouth and inside my body.

"Devin, wait."

He shook his head. "Look down, baby." I did as he asked and noticed what he wanted me to see. Despite not knowing when he managed to sheath himself with a condom, he had done so. "Not doing anything that would make you want to walk away from me again." He thrust harder. "Never again, Vic."

"Promise?" I asked as he continued to hammer into me with a ferocity that we'd never had in our love making before.

"On my life, baby."

10

DEVIN

"Did you ever go see that movie?"

Victoria moved her head on my chest, so she was angled enough to look up and see me. Her golden hair flowed over my shoulder and down behind her in a silky waterfall, but every time she moved, even slightly, the scent of honeysuckle and vanilla hit me all over again. It felt like coming home. I knew it was something I missed when she wasn't in my life, but I hadn't realized how much until I had her back in my arms.

"No. I couldn't make myself go without you."

"It's still playing in Brockton." Brockton was about an hour drive from home, in another county. It was one of the places we frequented for our dates because it was rare to run into anyone there. The only trouble was, we normally avoided the mall because that was the one place where we might be spotted by someone from our town. It also happened to be where the theater was located.

"Is that a hint?"

"I thought you might want to go see it with me today, since we both have off work."

"It's getting awfully close to the holidays to be seen in a mall together when you're married to someone else," She reminded me.

I couldn't help the involuntary sigh of frustration I let out.

"I didn't say, no. I guess we just need to be careful until we know for sure that everything will work out and that... You know," She finally said after a lengthy pause. It seemed as though my woman was back to not being able to speak about the baby that might be mine. Once again, fear zinged through me. What if I was wrong and the baby turned out to be mine? Would that truly be the end of Victoria and me?

"We will be careful, but Vic, I really don't think there is anything to worry about and I want to spend the day with you."

"Did you make her sign a prenup?"

That question was out of the blue, though I supposed it made sense, especially since Vic worked for a divorce attorney.

"Yes. I don't know if it will hold up in court. It was just something quick that was notarized by the same guy that married us."

She raised her head up and quirked a brow at me. "Your wedding officiant is also a notary?"

"It was that guy down on first street two blocks from the courthouse. He has to offer extra services because there aren't as many same-day weddings as they have in Vegas." I couldn't help but laugh as I remembered the guy telling me that.

"Virginia really needs to instate a waiting period. It might have saved you from making a huge mistake."

I shrugged my shoulders. "Probably, considering it took about twenty minutes to get the license and then ten minutes after we arrived at The Marriage Place, we signed the certificate and the guy printed out a fairly generic prenup for me when I asked that said the only assets either of us leave the marriage with are the ones we came into it with."

"It didn't state anything about money made during the marriage?" I shook my head. "Dumb," Vic huffed. "Don't ever get married without consulting me again."

"Don't plan on it."

We got up and got dressed after that because Vic wasn't really in a talking mood after having to discuss the marriage that never should have happened. She was right though, if there had been a waiting period to get married, I might have had time to talk myself out of doing it. The crazy thing was that I was always under the assumption that you had to go to Vegas for a quickie wedding. It was probably good that other people were ignorant to the fact that Vegas wasn't the only place in the country where you could get married on a whim in under an hour.

VICTORIA MIGHT HAVE BEEN RIGHT about it being too close to the holidays to go see a movie together in a theater that was located inside a shopping mall. Not that I would tell her, but I'd seen at least five people from our town since we arrived and we parked as close to the theater entrance as possible.

"I'm going to hit the ladies room while you get our snacks. Be right back!" Vic called out as she ran off to the bathrooms across the theater's lobby. There were two more people ahead of me, so I hoped Vic would make it back before I grabbed anything.

"Devin!" I turned at the sound of a very familiar voice and had to try really fucking hard not to lose my shit. Dallas headed my way with a giant grin on his face. "What's up man? Looks like we had the same idea. I tried to call to see if you wanted to come finally watch this thing before it left theaters, but I couldn't get a hold of you."

"To be honest, I'm avoiding my phone. There's a reason I headed over here." This was the best time to start planting the seeds of discontent between Justice and me, since Dallas thought we were a legitimate couple.

"The wifey on your ass to go get her pickles and ice cream or some shit?" He joked just as Victoria walked up. She must not have noticed him at first, but then her gasp at hearing her brother question me about Justice's pregnancy cravings and the wife bit caught her completely off guard.

"Vic?" Dallas questioned and then glanced back at me with narrowed eyes. "What are you doing here?"

"I was supposed to meet Jordan here, but she couldn't get away quickly enough, so I figured I'd catch a movie while I waited."

"Oh yeah? What are you going to see?" Victoria admitted she was here to see the same movie and Dallas once again had his head on a swivel looking between the two of us.

"Hey, Devin!" Vic offered cheerfully, as if she had just now noticed me. "I saw you up here and thought you might help me cut the concession line." The last bit was said in a mock-whisper as she leaned in conspiratorially. "Now, since Dallas is here too, I guess my little brother can buy my concessions."

"Sure thing, Sis." Dallas wasn't an idiot. He was suspicious about the two of us being here together, but he hadn't said a word yet.

I glanced at Victoria, looking for confirmation that it was okay to tell him about us, but she shook her head and then started to run her mouth about having heard lots of good things about the movie we had come to see together.

"We should all sit together, since we're here for the same show," Dallas suggested after we got our drinks and snacks. True to her request, my best friend bought his sister's stuff and I got my own. Our date had officially been hijacked by the unknowing best friend/brother. It wasn't the first time it had happened, but it sucked this time because it was like fate was throwing it in our faces that there were too many moving parts, and far too many challenges to us making everything work out as a couple.

I hoped like hell that I was wrong, but we had been happy earlier today and that happiness was dimming by the second with

Dallas in tow. It dimmed even further when he insisted on sitting between us like some 1800s chaperone.

Victoria mouthed, "Sorry" to me as she took her seat and her brother slid into the seat between us. I wished like hell I hadn't turned my cell phone off to avoid all the messages Justice left on my phone while I was with Victoria. Then we would have had a head's up about Dallas coming to the theater to see the same damn movie. I was damned if I do and if I don't with my best friend when it came to the woman who roped me into marrying her. Truthfully, if this shit kept up, I'd probably be damned lucky if Vic even looked at me again, let alone followed through with our plan to be together out in the open sooner than later.

11

VICTORIA

"Should have seen that movie last month when it first came out," Dallas mentioned as we all got up and shuffled out of the theater. What in the hell were we supposed to do? There was no way my brother would leave us alone until we were all in our cars on the way back home. The problem with that was I rode here with Devin and Dallas couldn't know that yet.

Thankfully, my phone dinged with an incoming text from Jordan as we made our way out to the mall again.

> Jordan: I hate this! She claimed to be pregnant and has him hooked. He had no qualms about telling me that he would help raise a baby if we had one together, but that didn't mean we had to be a couple. For her - he bends over backward to try to make her believe they can work it out. What did I do wrong?

> Victoria: I'm not sure what's going on. It feels like I missed several memos about what's going on with Austin lately.

Jordan: For sure, you've been caught up with your own drama. I'll fill you in tomorrow, if you're going to be home.

Victoria: I'll be there.

Jordan: Great see you then. He's here. He showed up. I'll let you know what happened.

Well shit. I was about to ask her to come get me, but that was out of the question since my brother was at her place. She would never turn down time with him, especially if it had gotten more complicated with the other woman. Jordan needed time to work out whatever was going on between her, my brother, and the other girl he kept going back to since their college days. It sounded like their situation was quickly becoming as awful as my own, and I didn't wish that on anyone.

"I'll walk you to your car." I looked up to see my brother and Devin both staring at me.

"Sorry, what?" I asked.

"I said, it's getting late and I will walk you to your car. You know how assholes get this time of year. No need to make yourself a victim." Dallas held his hand out, as if to offer me to go in front of him so I could lead the way to wherever I parked.

Holy shit, this was really happening. Either we had to come clean or I would have to find some way to get a ride an hour back to my house.

"Um," I held up my phone and waved it in the air for some asinine reason. "I told you I was meeting Jordan here, remember?"

"Yeah, but she's still not here."

"That was her. She's only a few minutes away."

"Maybe I should wait for her to show up." Dallas would not give up.

"Yeah, are you sure she's going to make it?" Devin asked. I

could see the worry in his eyes. He knew as well as I did that if I couldn't find another ride home, we would have to explain every-thing to Dallas, and we simply weren't ready for that, since Dev didn't have proof of what Justice had been up to yet.

"I swear, she just told me she was almost here. You guys can head out and don't worry about me. I won't be on my own." I smiled brightly and hoped like hell it looked far more genuine than it felt. A little panic started to rise in my chest at the thought of being stranded at the mall, an hour from home, on my own. We were close to the holidays when the crimes ramped up and when I went to the bathroom, there were posters with hotline numbers to call if you were a victim of human trafficking. To say I was freaked out to be on my own was an understatement, but I was equally freaked out about my baby brother finding out about the messy situation Devin and I managed to get ourselves into.

By the time I convinced the guys to leave me on my own, the sun had already started to set. I glanced around and bit my lip nervously as I pulled up a ride share app on my phone. I wasn't stupid. Most of the drivers wouldn't accept a ride that far as it would add too many miles to their vehicles and wouldn't pay out enough. I had to hope that at least one would take my offer.

Eventually, nearly fifteen minutes after my brother and Devin left, I finally found someone who would take the ride. By the time I got home, I was out nearly $200 and the same old worries started to circle in the back of my mind again. It felt like the universe pushed me to see that Devin and I were not meant to be. Why else would it be so damn hard?

12

DEVIN

DALLAS SIGNALED THAT HE NEEDED TO PULL INTO THE GAS station, which was good because I followed him and the fucker decided to take the scenic ride back. I figured I would gas up too and send a text to Vic to see if I needed to double back and come to get her. Unfortunately, when I pulled my phone out, the damn thing was so freaking dead it wouldn't even turn on. I ran into the gas station and came back out with a charger that would work in my car and plugged it in.

Dallas was still there and his brother Austin had pulled in while I was inside the store as well. "What's up?" I asked as I ducked into my car to plug the phone in.

"Austin was ranting about women when he pulled up," Dallas informed me. "What's going on with you and Becs now?"

"Not Becs. Jordan."

"Thought you were dating Becs again?"

"Yeah, I was until Jordan told me she was pregnant."

Dallas narrowed his eyes as he glanced my way. "That particular affliction seems to be going around a lot lately."

"More than you know. Becs is also pregnant."

"Fuck dude," Dallas hissed and I checked out of the conversation as I worried about how Vic was doing. I needed my phone to charge faster before I knocked both of the Mercer brothers out and took off after her anyway. If Austin was here dealing with Jordan's shit, then that meant the chances she had gone to meet up with my girl were slim to none.

Dallas must have had the same thought because he asked when Austin was with Jordan last.

"I just came from her place," Austin stated.

"She lied," Dallas growled. "Did she even have her car there?" He glared at me as he asked the question. "What the hell is going on with you and my sister?"

"Whoa! What sister? You better not be fucking around with Katy, asshole." Austin yelled.

Dallas laughed, but it was a menacing sound that put me on my guard. "No, that would be too easy and far more age appropriate, wouldn't it?" My best friend asked.

Before I could answer, Dallas's phone pinged with an incoming text. I was able to see it when he opened it up and there was a picture of my girl giving a thumbs up to the camera.

"You're lucky she said she's home now and that she didn't bother waiting around for Jordan."

"I'm lucky?" I asked.

"Yeah, fucker. Something isn't right between the two of you, and it better not be what I think because you're fucking married. It might be to Satan in makeup and a dress, but that little devil woman is carrying your child and I won't have my sister dragged into that bullshit."

"Damn Dallas, chill out. If something was going on between Victoria and your BFF, we would have known about it."

"You would think," Dallas murmured and then he turned and moved to get into his car. "I don't like being kept in the dark and I have a bad fucking feeling."

I wanted to tell him the truth. There was no need to keep it a secret besides the fact that I didn't have solid proof about the baby yet, but it wouldn't be long before I could get that. Still, I couldn't come clean to Dallas and Austin without talking to Victoria first. When I glanced at my phone again, Dallas slammed his car door shut and took off half a minute later.

"Look man, I get that life can be complicated, but I have to say, I rooted for you and Vic a couple years ago."

"What?" I asked Austin in shock. He nodded as if he figured it would be news to me that he knew about us.

"I hoped you two worked out whatever made you want to keep your relationship a secret, but then Justice was in the picture and I figured I didn't know shit about shit." Austin glanced back to where we could both see Dallas' taillights growing smaller in the distance.

"I don't know what the hell is happening now because my dumbass brother seems to think you married that bitch and maybe have a baby on the way. If that's the case, then you need to leave my sister alone. That kind of complicated bullshit is too much for anyone to handle. Vic comes off as strong and some-times domineering, being the oldest sibling and all, but she's all soft and gooey inside. I don't want to see my marshmallow of a sister display those soft insides to the people who cracked through the outer shell only to watch the good parts spill out and leave a mess behind."

I stood there speechless as Austin walked off, got in his own car, and took off without any further fanfare, just like his younger brother had done moments ago.

I needed a plan to get Justice out of our lives once and for all. If Victoria's brothers' attitudes were anything to go by, that plan needed to fall into place yesterday.

After I got in my car, I pulled my phone up and saw that it had enough charge to turn back on. The minute it was up and running again, I dialed Vic. The phone rang out to voicemail and did so again when I hung up and attempted another call.

"Vic, I know you got home safe, but we are never doing that

again. Your safety is more important than our secret or how someone might react to what has been going on. I wanted to come by and see you, but since you're not answering, I'm going to go home and work on getting my plan in place to get us out from under this mess with Justice. I love you. Please, remember that. I almost told your brothers today, but I didn't want to make another misstep without talking to you first."

"YOU OWE ME A DATE!" Justice snapped at me the minute I walked through the door.

"What the fuck?" I growled back.

Justice flounced toward me before even a single toe could get through my front door. If I didn't know better, I'd swear she had been lying in wait for me to get home. As soon as she was within reach, she slammed the door shut behind me and then stuck her hip out with her hand on it.

"What do you think you're doing?" My fake wife asked with just as much attitude as she had greeted me with.

"Last I checked, I'm a grown man and you aren't my mom. I don't have to answer to you."

"I AM YOUR WIFE!" She spat the words at me as if they were laced with venom and could do maximum harm on impact.

"We both know our marriage isn't real, so again, I don't know who you think you're yelling at, but this is my fucking house and I don't have to stand for it."

"Again, I am your wife and you don't have to stand for it, but this house will be mine in the divorce."

I laughed at Justice and the notion that I might owe her a damn thing. "You forgot that we signed a prenup."

The evil grin on her face should have been warning enough, but it didn't fully prepare me for what was coming.

"Oh? You mean the prenup that you never bothered to take to the clerk of court's office to file away for safe keeping?"

I glanced toward my bedroom where I kept all my important papers in a safe. There was no way she could get into that. Her smirk grew into a full-blown evil grin as if she could read my mind and was about to disabuse me of the notion that I had one up on her.

"You are more predictable than a watch, asshole. Your safe code was Victoria's birthday. My present for knowing that was to find the prenup and toss it in the fire." I glanced to the living room, where there was indeed a fire that seemed to be dying out. "Since you didn't think to make copies or file it with the court, you can't prove there was ever a prenup. Now, I'm going to ask you again where the hell you have been. You didn't come home at all last night and my parents stopped by to invite us out to dinner."

"That sounds like a personal problem." I threw the words at her along with my sneer as I turned back to the safe that was still wide open. The little bit of emergency money I normally kept in there, about $5,000, was notably missing.

"You can't just disappear to be with your ex-girlfriend. We are married and I am pregnant. What if something happened to the baby and I had an emergency."

"Seeing as to how you're standing here harassing me, that wish wasn't granted." It was a cold thing to say, but Justice plucked my last fucking nerve with her bullshit. I sifted through all my important papers. Nothing else was missing, but that didn't mean much. One thing that did catch my eye was our marriage certificate. Something itched at the back of my mind about it in conjunction with the prenup, but before the thought could fully form, I was hit with a fucking shoe.

I turned a hate-filled glare on Justice as she wound her arm back, ready to lob another high heel at my back. "Put it down or I will have you arrested for domestic abuse."

"Who would believe you?" She shouted the question at me as she patted her belly, as if that made her seem innocent.

I pointed to the corner of my room. "The video footage speaks for itself. Just like it will when I explain how you broke into my personal safe, stole important legal documents out, destroyed them, and helped yourself to my emergency stash of $20,000."

"There was only $5,000 in that safe!" She didn't think before the correction slipped from her mouth.

"So you acknowledge that the amount you stole from me is constituted as a felony theft in Virginia?" I questioned. It was my turn to smirk at her.

She laughed, but I didn't miss the panic beneath the sound. "We're married. What's yours is mine."

"We had a prenup that stated otherwise," I assured her.

"Prove it."

"No need. That camera isn't the only one in this house. You readily admitted to burning the prenup. The cameras caught you stealing it from my safe, throwing it into the fire, and gloating to me about how you did it. You admitted on camera that we had a prenup. I don't need more proof than that."

She screamed out her frustration at me. "You will take me to dinner tomorrow night, in public. You will pretend to be happy with me at first, where my parents can see us. Then, we'll fake a massive fight, so they won't be blindsided when I have to move back in with them until I convince Brody to get me my own place. If you do that, and play along for another month or so, I will give you the annulment you want."

Something like pure evil shined in Justice's eyes and I didn't trust her for one fucking second. "Fine," I agreed. It would make things easier on me.

"In return, you will give me those tapes."

It was my turn to laugh. "No, I don't think I will. We'll call those tapes my collateral. And before you get any ideas, they download to a protected server that is not in this house. They also download to cloud storage, so even if you knew where the server was, you would never get your hands on every copy."

"You will be on your best behavior tomorrow night!" She shouted as she stomped off to her own bedroom.

I closed my door and locked it, worried that the bitch would try to kill me in my sleep if I gave her the opportunity. I pulled my cell out and tried to call Victoria again. She needed to know about the date I had coming up with Justice. Once again, she didn't answer her phone, so I sent a quick text.

> Devin: Something happened. I wanted to explain, but keep getting sent to voicemail. I have to go out on a date with Justice tomorrow. I am going to cause a scene with her, so everyone - who isn't our family - will know we are headed for Splitsville. I want us to tell our families everything. I love you. Don't forget that.

I didn't bother to wait for a response. I needed food, a shower, and a good night's sleep to help me deal with the crazy bitch who lived in my house.

13

VICTORIA

AFTER A HARD NIGHT OF SLEEP, I FINALLY PICKED UP MY PHONE AND took a look at it. I don't know why I thought Devin didn't care. The phone message he left mentioned my brother taking them on the scenic route back and that his phone died with no charger in the car. I turned to stare guiltily at my purse, where I'd accidentally stuffed his charger cord because it was still attached to my phone when we got out of the car.

By the time Devin got it charged, I had already sent a message to my brother with picture proof that I made it home safely. I knew he would have come back for me. I knew he never wanted to leave and if I hadn't lied to him, he would have explained everything to Dallas then and there. Part of me wanted that, but the other part of me wanted to be sure that we weren't in for a lifetime of complications dealing with Justice first. I glanced down at my phone again and pulled up the text he left for me the night before.

Devin: Something happened. I wanted to explain, but keep getting sent to voicemail. I have to go out on a date with Justice tomorrow. I am going to cause a scene with her, so everyone - who isn't our families - will know we are headed for Splitsville. I want us to tell our families everything. I love you. Don't forget that.

Victoria: Sorry. Fell asleep last night with phone off. Let me know how the dinner goes. I am going to catch up with Jordan today. She seemed upset with my brother yesterday.

Devin: Yeah, he told us that she was very upset with him about five minutes before he rolled up on us at the gas station. You lied. Do not ever put yourself in danger again to keep our secret.

I hadn't expected an immediate response to my text, but Devin was right. I had gone to bed angry with him for leaving me there. Even though I knew it was stupid to feel that way. It was my own damn fault. I just felt so out of control whenever other people were around us. It's like fight or flight responses kicked in every time and I let my panic make the decisions, even when I knew it wouldn't turn out for the best.

Not for the first time, I thought it might be worthwhile to go get some therapy. If things were going to work out between Devin and me, I had to come to grips with everything that scared me about our relationship, starting with the age difference and moving on to how to not care about other people's judgements.

I glanced down at my phone again and responded to Devin's text, while I hoped my answer wouldn't end up being a lie.

Victoria: I know. It won't happen again.

After I sent the last text to Devin, I got up and started to get ready for my day. I wasn't sure what to do with myself. It was

Sunday. I could always go to my family's house for brunch, but I hadn't made it a habit of going there over the past two years because of all the questions about my supposed lack of a dating life. Every time I was around my family, they had questions for me that there were no honest answers to. Thinking back on it, I realized I destroyed a little bit of my relationship with the family for the sake of my secret relationship with Devin and that was one more point that should probably be talked through with a therapist.

Why had I been so willing to throw my family to the wayside and keep Devin hidden? The whole point in the secret relationship was because I thought my family might disown me for dating a younger man - my little brother's best friend. I ended up basically disowning them instead. I had no clue what was going on in my brothers' lives. Devin had mentioned something about Houston being in a serious relationship, something my sister had informed me of as well. I still hadn't met the girl. Then there was the whole drama going on with Jordan, and something there wasn't adding up.

> Victoria: Are you free at all today?

I sent the text out to Jordan because I knew what it was like to have to watch the man you loved give his time to another woman. She would need a good friend to talk to because in all honesty, Austin had never claimed her as a girlfriend for a reason. I knew all about their on and off again fuck buddy situation. I knew she hoped he would come around eventually and make it more. Considering they worked together and spent an inordinate amount of time together outside of work, I thought they were finally headed in that direction too.

Like a coward, I hadn't bothered to contact my brother because meddling in his business meant he could meddle right back in mine. While he might have been oblivious to what was going on in his own personal life, I didn't think he was that blind to what had been going on in mine.

Thankfully, he hadn't butted in and I wanted to give him the same grace, although it felt as though someone needed to step in for Jordan's sake because she was like family to all of us. It wasn't okay for my brother to keep her dangling on his hook while he waited around to see if a bigger, better fish caught the line too.

> Jordan: How about dinner tonight? I could really use a friend.

> Victoria: You got it. Pick your poison and let me know. We can meet up here or at whichever restaurant you choose.

> Jordan: We can meet at the restaurant. How about Fredrick's? I get off work at five, since I'm doing inventory, and can walk right over.

> Victoria: See you at 5.

THE MINUTE we walked into Frederick's, I knew it was the wrong place to be. I couldn't leave though because that would make a scene we weren't ready for.

"I'm so sorry," Jordan whispered. "Do you want to leave? I don't think they've seen us yet."

I shook my head. "Trust me, the bitch noticed the minute I walked through the door. If I leave now, people will wonder why."

"You are a braver bitch than I am. Not sure I could sit through watching your brother on a date with his whore."

I turned to see the absolute hatred that flashed across Jordan's face as she mentioned Becs. I wish I knew the whole story there. I wasn't naive enough to think that Jordan's story was the full picture. If I hadn't kept myself so estranged from my family, I might know more. That was something I would have to rectify later, but it couldn't happen before we sat down to dinner. In the meantime, I would be there for Jordan while I tried to distance myself from the fact that our table would have a perfect view of the love of my life on a date with his fucking wife.

"So, what's going on with you and Austin?"

Jordan's face turned sour as she set the menu aside. "I think I messed up."

"Yeah, you did, when you put up with just being a convenience to my brother."

Jordan scowled at me for a minute and then shook her head, as if she had to bite off whatever retort she had for me. I didn't miss the way her eyes traveled the distance to where my man sat with another woman, though. She made her point quietly. The Mercer siblings seemed to have a problem with diving into straight forward relationships. We oozed into muddied waters and then bemoaned the drama our situations caused instead.

"I really need you to be here for me, Vic. The rest of your family is so angry with me."

That caught my attention. "What do you mean?"

"I screwed up."

"What did you do?"

"I-" She choked back whatever she'd been about to say as her eyes grew wide. I turned my head just enough to see Justice slip her forkful of food into Devin's mouth. He smiled around the fork so sweetly that if I didn't know the whole story, I would think they were a loved up newlywed couple expectantly awaiting the birth of their... Nope. Couldn't go there.

"Shit, we should leave," Jordan offered again. I was about to agree with her when the server came over.

"Ma'am, there are two men at the hostess station who say they're here for you," the hostess stated.

"Me?" I questioned.

"Crap, I forgot about them. Please, don't be mad, but I wanted to make Austin jealous."

I glanced over at the hostess station where two men stood eyeing up our table. TWO MEN. "Are they both your dates?" I asked in a tone that begged her to say they were.

Jordan shook her head. "I heard Dallas mention that Devin and his wife would be here."

"You knew, and still brought me here anyway?" I wanted to shout at her, but managed to ask the question through clenched teeth instead.

"Please, just let's make the most of it. Look," Jordan pointed toward the table where Dev sat with his wife. He leaned over a bit and used his thumb to swipe away whatever food had gathered on her lips. He stared at her mouth as if he wanted to devour it and that was when I made up my mind.

The last time he thought I had gone out on a date with someone else, he got drunk and slept with that bitch, which was why they were married now. I wanted him to have to see me on a date with another man while he was acting all lovey-dovey with the whore who came between us. Their dinner was supposed to be a breakup scene, not honeymoon bliss.

I nodded my head to Jordan and the nervous hostess went back to grab our dates and escort them to us. "Just so you know, Mark knows what's going on tonight. I told him the gist of the issues with Devin and he agreed to be your date and cause drama, but he knows it won't go anywhere."

I nodded my head, even though I was once again angry with Jordan because she took it upon herself to tell a complete stranger about my embarrassing situation. She must have caught the anger simmering beneath the surface of my fake calm, because she apologized.

"Sorry, I thought it would be better than leading him on and you having to fend off grabby hands and expectations."

"We'll talk about it later, Jordan. I'm not a fan of being blind-sided and I thought you wanted to talk about the mess with Austin, since you somehow managed to anger my whole family while I'm in the dark about it."

She had the sense to look chagrined as the men approached the table. My surprise date for the night held his hand out to me. "Hi, I'm Mark."

"Victoria," I answered back as he took the seat next to mine. I hadn't bothered to shake his hand and instead picked up my wine glass to take a fortifying drink for my jangled nerves.

"Jordan explained the situation, but I have to say, I'm disappointed that this isn't a real date. She didn't do your beauty justice when she described you."

I knew his use of the word "justice" was only a figure of speech, but it rubbed me the wrong way and sent my eyes trailing across the restaurant to see the bitch. Even though he had unknowingly mentioned her name, it was like she heard it. Our eyes met across the restaurant and she stared daggers in my direction. I couldn't bring myself to look at Devin though. He could eat his heart out. I was tired of being the one who had to watch as his time with her played out like a beautiful relationship while I was relegated to the shadows - even if I'd put my own damn self there.

"Thank you. I honestly don't know why you signed yourself up for this."

He chuckled. "Truthfully, I was trying to be a good wingman. My friend has had a thing for Jordan for a while now, but she's been too hung up on Austin to care."

"You know my brother?" I asked.

He cocked his beautifully bald head to the side and then showed off his brilliant white teeth as he smiled. "Ah, I see it now. I didn't realize the woman I would have to help out tonight was Austin's little sister."

I shook my head and laughed. "Not the little sister. That's Katy. I'm the oldest Mercer sibling."

"No fucking way." He shook his head adamantly. "I just turned thirty and there is no way you're almost my age and older than Houston."

"I promise you that I recently turned 29, so it is true." I was a bit taken aback at the mention of Houston. "Do you know all my brothers?" I asked.

"Yeah, I do. Houston and I were on the same community league baseball team before his bar renovations started to take up all his time."

"Oh."

"Why didn't I ever see you at the games?"

"I don't know. I guess there were other things taking all of my attention."

"Other things like the angry guy across the room who can't take his eyes off of you?"

My cheeks heated. "Yes, something like that."

"Jordan told me you had a secret relationship. Why would anyone ever want to keep you in the dark and flaunt that bitch around instead?"

"It started out as my fault. He's younger than me, and I was not ready for all the judgement for dating my baby brother's best friend."

"Oh. Well, fuck that. If he was any kind of man, he would have told you it was all or nothing."

"He had been trying to get me to date him for a year, I don't think he was ready to give up so easily."

"Seems to me he already made his choice and it was the wrong girl."

"What makes you say that?"

"Those two are wearing wedding bands, sweetheart. Nothing says it's over quite like your lover committing to someone else legally."

He wasn't wrong, and it made me wonder where Devin had gotten another wedding band so fast, considering the last one was still lost somewhere on my kitchen floor. With the realization of how determined he was to look the part of a happily married couple, when he claimed they were supposed to be staging a breakup scene, I made a decision to say, "Fuck Devin!".

I didn't say no when Mark asked if I'd like to go to the dance floor with him. To hell with food. I told Jordan to order me something light, took Mark's hand, and followed him out to the area that was cleared for a dance floor. It was one of the quirks of Frederick's. The owner and his wife often had impromptu dances in front of all the customers. They also hosted an annual swing dance competition that they closed the restaurant down for once a year.

The only other couple on the dance floor was an elderly pair who had to be in their late 70s. They smiled indulgently at us as Mark spun me around and clasped our hands together on one side while his other hand wrapped around my trim waist. I hadn't worn anything special, since I didn't know I'd be walking into a blind date. Still, I had on a blue silk blouse and black dress slacks because Frederick's was a place where you tried to look your best.

"The ones who aren't afraid to take you dancing in the middle of a restaurant are the keepers," the old woman told me and followed it up with a sly wink.

The tempo picked up and Mark swung me out in a surprise move that made me throw my head back and laugh as he then tugged and spun me back into his bubble. "God, you're beautiful." He whispered as my eyes came up to lock with his. "Devin is a fool."

Of course he knew who Devin was. The fact that Jordan had spilled my secrets to a man who obviously knew all of my brothers, and my secret boyfriend of two years, felt even more like a betrayal. It made me wonder, once again, what she had done to piss my family off. I would get it out of her eventually, along with another lengthy apology for putting me in this position and spilling my secrets.

Mark spun me out and back again and by the time I was in his arms again, there was another couple dancing beside us. It didn't even register who it was until the woman spoke to me.

"Fancy seeing you here with a date," Justice snapped at me with a vicious tone. I ignored the bitch, but then Devin leaned in close. "What are you doing on a date?"

"What are you doing being hand fed by that bitch and having the time of your fucking life?" I countered as I purposely stared down at his left hand that rested on Justice's shoulder. The wedding band winked in the light, as if to emphasize my pointed look.

Justice pulled on Devin, so he couldn't answer right away. She turned and slid her backside down his front and made sure that I could see the full-body contact they had going on. Devin took a step back, but far too late.

As I lifted an accusatory brow in his direction, his eyes scanned me and my date. The frown line on his forehead creased deeper as he seemed to notice the respectful space between my body and Mark's. Our hands were the only parts that touched besides where my other hand was placed on his shoulder and his just above my right hip.

There was nothing intimate about our dance whereas Justice had once again moved into Devin's space and pulled his arms around her middle to rest his hands on her belly. She wanted to send a message to me and it was received painfully. Devin glanced down and pulled his hands back immediately, but the damage was already done. To add insult to my injury, the older lady on the dance floor loudly announced her congratulations to the expecting couple.

"You know what? I'm not feeling very well. I think I'm just going to go."

"If you ever get shy of him, and want to try this for real, give me a call."

"Sure," I whispered. "Do me a favor?" He nodded.

I glanced back at Devin - who looked like someone just kicked his puppy - and Justice - who wore a smug smile that made me want to punch her right in the nose. "Don't ever hook up with that bitch." I pointed to Justice, who continued to stare at me before she noticed my date and ogled him as if Devin wasn't right there by her side wearing a wedding ring that tied them together. Their "breakup date" was apparently important enough for him to get a replacement ring. Then again, I hadn't seen a single sign of an impending breakup all night.

"She's got trouble and gold digger stamped all over her. Rest assured that would never happen, but I meant what I said about wanting a chance with you."

"I don't think I'm ready to spread my dating wings again just yet."

Mark glanced back over his shoulder again. "Somehow, I think that's coming sooner rather than later. I can be patient."

14

DEVIN

WHAT IN THE ABSOLUTE FUCK JUST HAPPENED?

My mind felt like it exploded right alongside my heart. How in the hell was it possible that Jordan and Victoria came to this restaurant for dinner? I glanced over at the table as Vic grabbed her purse and headed for the door. The smug look on Jordan's face told me she was responsible for everything. From Vic being here to the double date that had been arranged for the two of them. I probably had Dallas to thank for the bitch having the info. He asked what I was up to this evening and I told him about 'date night' at Frederick's.

Stupid fucking shit. Worse, was that as I looked around, it was obvious that Justice's parents were not here, so our little show was for nothing. Not for nothing, as it served to destroy another frayed string that held my relationship with Vic in place. I watched as she walked out of the restaurant with her date not far behind.

"Stop staring at her, people are starting to notice."

"You set this up, didn't you?"

"How would I know where your stupid little schoolboy crush was going to be tonight?" She laughed lightly. "Seems to me, she came to verify a few things for herself and you played the part of my doting husband so well, she believed you." Justice smacked my shoulder playfully and then moved to leave the dance floor. She made sure to keep her hand on her belly the whole time, emphasizing the growing baby bulge beneath her too-tight dress.

What she didn't realize was that by showing off her bump, she made it that much more obvious that the baby couldn't be mine. She also didn't realize that it finally occurred to me just how important her burning the only copy of the prenup was. It finally sunk in, but there were a few loose strings I needed to tie together before I unleashed holy hell on the bitch.

Before that could happen, I needed to get the fuck out of Frederick's and go find my woman. There was no way in hell I was going to leave her with the impression that there was more between Justice and me than loathing at this point. In the beginning, we'd been friends out of circumstance. That didn't even exist any longer, despite what Vic thought she saw between us.

By the time I informed Justice that she could pay the bill and find her own way home, I knew I was running short on time to get to Vic before she shut down and shut me out completely. There was also the real problem that I was angry with her for being on a date with another man. We promised one another we were done playing games. I barely bothered to park properly on the road in front of Vic's house before I jogged up to the door and banged my fist against it.

The minute she cracked the door open, I barged in without giving her the chance to shut it in my face. "I'm sorry. Her parents were supposed to be there in the restaurant. We were supposed to put on this show-"

"Oh, you put on quite the show for the whole town, but it wasn't the one you mentioned in the text you sent me." Vic's tone remained calm, if slightly sarcastic, as she spoke. That was not a good sign.

"We were supposed to start out as a normal couple and then have a fight."

"Is that right? So you were cool with eating off the same fucking fork that bitch had in her mouth not two seconds before?"

"No, I wasn't, but..."

"Or how about when you looked so lovingly at her while you wiped away the remnants of her meal from her lips? Was that supposed to start a fucking fight, Devin?"

"Vic, please, if you'd let me explain..."

"You know what? No!"

"What?"

"Just what I said. I'm tired of your explanations, Dev. There comes a point when they stop meaning shit, except to highlight that you don't care how bad you make things look before we supposedly go public. Did you stop, for one fucking second, to think that a show like that - whether it ended in a fight or not - would make people believe the two of you were in love and I was the problem in the middle?"

I didn't know what to say. Every argument I had fell to the wayside as Vic made her point. Justice had been a step ahead of me all along, except with my most recent realization, but that was something I would discuss with Vic after I managed to convince her to calm down and hear me out. She had no clue about the burned prenup, the video cameras in my house, or the deal I thought I'd made with Justice the night before to end everything.

"I felt like throwing up when I sat there and watched you do those things with her. You're an amazing actor, Dev because I believed it. My stomach almost emptied on the dance floor when you let her rub all over you, but you didn't even notice how sick I looked. You didn't even notice that Mark and I barely touched one another while your date..." She cut herself off with a harsh laugh. "No, your wife, slid her body all along yours and pulled you in to hug her and hold her baby bump in front of me. I wanted to die while you just stood there and made me watch."

"It wasn't like that, Vic. I was in fucking shock that you were out with another man."

"Well, the difference between us was that you planned to go play happy families in public with Justice. Mark was foisted on me by Jordan without me knowing until he and his buddy showed up at the restaurant." I watched as Vic shook her head. "You told me that your dinner with her was supposed to be a staged fight and all anyone in that restaurant saw was the two of you all loved up on one another and happily sharing a meal."

"That's not all they saw. Everyone in that restaurant watched as I put Justice in her place for setting that whole thing up. Her parents were supposed to be there and they never showed. Miraculously, your friend took you to the restaurant where we were supposed to have our breakup scene. I don't feel as though that was a coincidence either. The rest of the diners in that restaurant watched as I yelled at her and then left to come to you. Christ, I didn't even pay for her meal." What I didn't mention was that I told Justice she could pay for it out of the money she stole from me the night before.

"I don't want to hear it anymore, Devin. I'm tired of feeling like the second choice, and barely that."

"I swear to you, Vic, you are the only choice."

"Sure, it really felt like that when you caressed her lips in front of me."

"What about when that asshole had you laughing on the dance floor? You didn't think that gutted me?"

"I wouldn't know because you were too busy dirty dancing with your pregnant wife."

"It's not my fucking baby and she isn't my wife!" I yelled at her because my temper decided it wouldn't be held at bay anymore, even if it was directed at the wrong person.

Vic pointed at my hand and laughed. "Funny, you even managed to snag another ring to prove to everyone just how untrue that statement is. You went out of your way to wear a wedding band tonight. I know you had to get one especially to prove something, because I have the other one you threw in my house last time you tried to tell me your marriage meant nothing. That's what you said when you threw the last ring, that it didn't mean anything. You sure did scramble to get a replacement before you were seen in public without one."

I snatched the new ring off my finger too. "She handed this to me before we left the house." Justice hadn't missed the fact that my wedding band was missing from my finger. She had demanded that I put it back on before we left and when I told her it was gone, she held up another one. I didn't want to put it on, but then figured it could be part of the breakup scene, and I could leave the ring with her. Only that shit hadn't gone quite to plan.

"Before you left..." She paused and stared up into my eyes as tears welled in hers. "The house you live in, with your pregnant wife," Vic replied in a cold, detached tone I'd never heard her use before. "Right. Well, you should go home to your wife because she's your problem. You know who isn't your problem anymore? ME."

"Vic, I love you!"

"Get the fuck out of my house, Devin!" The harsh way she yelled those words at me made me stumble to a stop before I could reach for my woman. She threw her hands up in the air, almost in surrender, except they were used to hold me at arm's length in the most literal manner. "I mean it. Get out of my house. We are done."

"We're not done," I pleaded, but she simply pointed at the door.

"Go before I call someone to remove you."

I wasn't sure if she meant her brothers or the law, but I turned and walked to the door. "We're not done, Vic. There are things you don't know…"

"There's plenty I don't know," she sassed back. "Us being finished is crystal fucking clear though."

15

VICTORIA

I WASN'T SURE IF I WAS SEEING THINGS OR IF GOD REALLY HATED me. Once I blinked a few times to clear my vision, the sight before me remained the same.

Across the street, seated at an outdoor cafe, was my ex-boyfriend with his wife and parents, having a happy little family feast. If there was ever any doubt about how he felt for me, it was alleviated as I watched him laughing and carrying on with all of them as if life was absolutely brilliant. So much for their faux breakup at the restaurant. I suppose me pushing him out my door and telling him it was over between us changed things.

It made me sad to think that I'd cried myself to sleep while he apparently went home and made up with the she-bitch-from-hell. It shouldn't hurt, since I was the one to tell him we were over, but it did. It sliced me to the point where all I could do was bleed out the pain.

There he sat, across the street, looking happier than ever with his current situation. It had been three days of radio silence since I kicked him out of my place. Three days seemed to have a huge impact on his life. Maybe I had been the burden holding him back all along. Devin was meant to shine with a woman his own age. His wife. His baby. The woman his family accepted without even the barest hint of her being beneath him. My heart cracked wide open once again, as if I hadn't already bled the stupid organ dry.

I was meant to go to my doctor appointment, in the office directly across the street from where they were all happily dining. There was no way I could make myself get out of the car, though. Instead, I picked up my phone and dialed the office I was parked in front of. Figures, the one time I got prime parking, and I'd have to give it up because I couldn't get out of my car.

"Dr. Mitchell's office," The sweet voice on the other end of the line answered.

"Hi, this is Victoria Mercer. I need to cancel my appointment today."

"Oh no, is everything okay?"

"I'm not feeling well. I think it's safer if I stay home in case I have something you guys might catch from me." The sniffles I couldn't hold back any longer most likely lent credence to my story. "I don't want to be responsible for the staff, or heaven forbid a pregnant woman, ending up with the flu." I narrowed my eyes on the one pregnant woman I wished would fall down a never-ending flight of stairs as I said that.

"Aww, I wish all our patients were that considerate. Okay, did you want to go ahead and reschedule or wait and see how quickly you recuperate?"

"I'll just wait and call back when I'm feeling better."

"That's fine. I do need to remind you that you were supposed to get your birth control shot during this appointment. You will need to be careful and use a backup birth control method until you can get back in to see us."

I laughed as another fissure was added to my heart. "Trust me, that won't be an issue. Thanks for everything. Sorry for the late notice." I hung up after babbling and didn't wait for her to say anything else. Instead, I started my car again and checked my blind spot to see if it was okay to pull out. As I swiveled back around to face front, my eyes caught movement. Justice's finger extended in my direction as Devin nearly stood all the way up from his seat before his father yanked his arm to get him to sit back down. I pulled away before I could see anything else.

Maybe they knew about us the way Katy had known. It was clear by Devin's father's actions that he didn't approve of me. It was also clear that they loved his wife. My stomach twisted into a tight knot as that word embedded itself onto another fissure in my heart. Instead of stitching the wound closed, that word was placed there to hold it open. *Wife.* Devin had a wife and it wasn't me. My heart twisted inside my chest. It wasn't a metaphor. I could have sworn I felt the squeeze as my lungs attempted to gulp air down.

He seemed happy without me. There was no denying that the Devin I saw today was carefree and unburdened in a way he had never been with me by his side. I had seen a similar look at Frederick's as she fed him from her plate.

It wasn't a moment we had ever shared together. Then again, we had never been able to sit out in an open-air cafe, or any restaurant within an hour of where we lived, together. We certainly had never been able to openly - or privately for that matter - share a meal with any of our family. That was all my fault. I had turned our relationship into something dirty that needed to be hidden in the shadows. Devin must have come to the same conclusion. It was clear from how happy he appeared that our relationship was nothing more than a dark stain on the past two years. Openly dating his harpy of a wife looked like a relief in comparison to living in the shadows the way we had been.

I didn't bother to go back to work. Instead, I drove to my lonely little apartment, went straight to my bedroom and buried myself under the covers. Every woman with a broken heart deserved to wallow for a day, at least, after seeing her ex living his happily ever after with someone else. Life was unfair, and that thought was made worse by the fact that the misery I suffered was of my own making.

TWO HOURS LATER, I was awoken from a nap I hadn't realized I'd taken, by someone pounding on my door. By the time I made it down the stairs and to the door, the pounding started all over again.

"I know you're home. Your car is outside," Devin announced angrily.

I flipped the locks and slid the door open a smidge, but he was having none of that. The man pushed it open wider, and knocked me out of the way as he moved into my home. "What the hell, Devin?" I shrieked at him as I stumbled out of the way and tried to catch my footing before I fell.

He ignored me and turned to shut and lock the door again with him on the inside. "We're going to have a chat. Since you won't answer your phone, I guess we have to do this the hard way – in person."

I laughed at him. "It's hard to answer a phone that never rings."

"Bullshit! I've been calling every day, several times a day, since you kicked me out of your house three days ago. I've left voice messages and texts."

I moved over to the coffee table, where I'd thrown all my stuff down when I came back from the doctor appointment I never went to. My phone sat there, silent as the grave. I picked it up, unlocked it, and handed it over to Devin.

"What am I supposed to do with this?"

"Look at my texts and call history, asshole. Not that I need to prove to you that you haven't contacted me. Though, I do think it's cruel to lie to my face and say that you have. Considering I've cried myself to sleep every night while you've been off living your best life and enjoying happy family time, I guess I'm not sure why you came here to lie to my face. I realize you might want to punish me for all the time I kept our relationship a secret, but trust me when I say, having the love of my life impregnate and marry another woman is more than even I deserved. Being forced to watch as you get to play happy families with her on top of everything else is devastating. Just leave me alone, Devin. See yourself out after you verify what you already know - I never got a single call or text from you because you never sent any."

I turned and angrily stomped my way to the kitchen. I tried to give up coffee a couple days before my world turned upside down. Obviously, it was the wrong time to attempt caffeine withdrawal.

"All this proves is that you deleted them without looking at anything," Devin argued as he brought my phone back to me while I filled the pot.

"You cannot be that obtuse. I just told you I cried myself to sleep every night because after you left my place the other night, I never heard from you again. You couldn't even apologize to me. Not one single, "I'm sorry." If you were happier with her because it didn't have to be a secret, all you had to do was break things off with me officially. Instead, you had to cheat. Only," I laughed again, "it wasn't really cheating as far as anyone else knows, since they all thought she was your girlfriend, right? So, I can't even be mad publicly."

He stared at me as if I had two heads, but I carried on. "Then you had to keep stringing me along and pretending that our relationship was the one you really wanted. Honestly, I don't understand why you would do that to me. Why do you want to hurt me so badly?"

"In case you forgot, you're the one who wanted the secrets, not me."

"And now you're punishing me for that, even though you agreed it was for the best. You told me your parents wouldn't like our relationship. You were the one worried about losing your best friend too."

"I was worried about those things, but I told you we could handle them together. I agreed to a temporary secret relationship to make sure we were good together before we broke the news to everyone else. You're the one who refused to change that up. Then, when Dallas started to question things, it was your idea to have us both be seen on dates, which is how the whole thing with Justice was concocted."

"You're right." I told him as I stuffed far too many coffee grounds into the pot before I turned it on. Bold coffee today seemed about right. "I pushed you to cheat on me. I stood there and told her to hop on your lap and go to town and make a baby while she was at it. I practically walked you down the aisle to her!" The words screamed out of me as my frustration built. "There were rules in place! YOU broke those rules. *She* broke those rules. YOU broke my heart, not the other way around." We had already hashed all of this out, but those early decisions were at the core of my misery again, and they did not want to be shoved back into the box I tried to bury them in when I gave Dev a second chance.

"Look, we've been down that road already, and I thought we worked through it, but obviously not. I had no intention of coming here to hurt you more though, and I have tried to call and text you." Devin offered as he pulled his own phone out and unlocked it. Then he pulled up his text messages. He put his phone in my hand, and I scrolled back, looking at about five to ten texts per day for the past few days. I glanced up to see his angry glare and shook my head in disbelief.

"I never got any of these."

"Bullshit!" He yelled at me as he snatched his phone back and pulled up his call log. "Look!" He shouted at me again as he held the phone out for me to see. "I called and texted every day. Fuck! My boss damn near booted my ass out of the office because I was on my phone so much - and not to sell houses."

"Devin, if you need me to go pull up the records from my cell phone company, I can. I never received any of that."

"That's fucking impossible, unless you blocked me."

"Call me now," I suggested. He angrily stabbed at the phone and hit the call button. Nothing happened. I picked up my phone to show him that nothing was coming in. Then I called him. Nothing. It rang once on my end before going straight to voicemail.

"What the fuck?"

"You are the one who has me blocked!" My words came out on a gasp, as it registered that he had completely shut me out. Never mind the bullshit he tried to spew about how he had called and texted me. I don't know who he called or messaged, but it hadn't been me.

"I do not have you blocked. And why couldn't I get through to you?"

"Give me your phone." I held out my hand and he complied, but decided to invade my personal space as he crowded in beside me to see what I was looking for. I pulled up my personal contact sheet in his phone and then pushed the information button. Then, I pointed at what I saw there. "That is not my phone number." He took a solid step back and shook his head. "I don't know who you've been sending all those messages to, but it wasn't me. That's my name, but the phone number isn't right at all."

"I haven't changed anything. Your contact has always worked. Did you change your number?"

"No, I didn't. Maybe someone who had access to your phone changed it," I suggested.

"No one has..." Devin stopped mid-sentence and I could just imagine who might have access to his phone long enough to make it impossible for him to contact me without showing up in person.

"Let me guess, your wife decided that we should no longer be in contact now that she set her sights on you instead of the married man she was fucking."

"No. It's not like that. We're not together like that."

"Funny, but that's not how it looked this morning when I saw the two of you together having a meal with your parents."

"What were you doing there?" He asked in a clipped tone.

"I had a fucking doctor appointment that I couldn't even go to because I couldn't force myself to get out of the car and be seen by you after watching how happy your whole family was together."

My emotions got the better of me as I yelled the accusations at him. I'd like to blame the fact that I hadn't received my shot today, but I think the hormonal issue I was having had more to do with the broken heart than the birth control – or lack thereof.

"It wasn't like that, Vic."

"Wasn't it?" I asked.

"No, I swear. I told my parents the truth about everything. They know about you and what happened with Justice."

"Well, they seemed pretty happy with her and your dad made it very obvious he didn't want you coming after me."

Devin's shoulders slumped. "They're angry that I'm in this situation with a wife I don't want and a baby on the way that isn't mine. My parents blame you for putting me in a place where any of that was possible."

"They blame me? They blame me for your cheating and running off to marry a woman who claimed to be pregnant with your child before you could even ask any questions – like 'Is it mine?'."

"They blame you for being ashamed of me and making us a secret to begin with. Everything else, they put directly on my shoulders because I'm a fucking adult and I made the idiotic decisions I did all on my own. They blame both of us for the mess I have to make to set it all right."

"How do you know it's not your baby?" I asked when what he'd said a bit ago finally processed.

"Not that I didn't already suspect, but I saw her ultrasound picture and it confirmed some things for me. Considering we only had sex that once - maybe-"He scrunched his nose up on that last word

"Maybe?" I questioned.

"You know I don't remember. It still doesn't sit right with me that my body was able to get onboard when my brain was complete mush. I wish you had just stuck around that day when you first found out, so we could work everything out then."

"If you'd talked to me before running off to marry another fucking woman, maybe my initial reaction wouldn't have been to run, Devin! Jesus! How would you have felt if you came to my place and heard me talking to my brand new husband about a baby we made together? How would it make you feel to know that there would only be one way for a baby to be in the mix and that meant I was unfaithful?"

"It would fucking crush me." He admitted.

"Something like that," I agreed. "It broke me. You broke me!" I clutched at my heart as tears streamed down my face. He didn't understand what it felt like and he never would. There was no way I could ever put him in a similar situation. "I've been living in this weird bubble with you the past few weeks where I couldn't even acknowledge that there was a baby that might be yours. After not speaking to you for a few days, it all sunk in again. It's like a dam breaking after too much rain. It all came back full force this time."

"You don't think being your damn secret for two years hasn't broken me too?"

"I'm sure it has," I whispered in defeat, knowing it must have been heartbreaking at times to be with me, but never be seen with me. "I was wrong, and now there's no going back from where we are. We literally can't come clean with our secret."

"Why the hell not?"

"You are the one who is trapped in the situation with her, but you allowed your family to put the blame for that completely on my shoulders. It's funny how your parents just accepted her and the situation she's in, but they seem to think I'm the devil."

"They don't know who the father of her baby is." His admission nearly floored me. Why hadn't he told them that part? Why had he spared the dirty details when it came to her, but not me?

"Well, isn't that rich. I thought you told them the truth." I laughed and turned my back on the man I once loved. "I guess I'm the whipping boy in this situation, since I created it. I think you should leave now. You made it pretty clear where your loyalties lie and they're not with me."

"You went on a date with another man!" He yelled at me then, as if that one moment in our lives was the defining moment that changed everything. I knew better.

"No, I fucking didn't! My mother arranged a date for me and one of her friend's sons. I said I would go but made myself so sick about it that I ended up throwing up because of the anxiety swirling in my belly over going through with it. I never went on the stupid fucking date. I never kissed another man, never held his hand, never even said more than "Hello" to him. I certainly didn't wake up naked with anyone. I sure as fuck never had the potential of being pregnant by another man while we were together, and damn sure didn't get married to anyone else. You know who did ALL OF THOSE THINGS? You did!"

"I was talking about the other night."

I rolled my eyes at Devin. "Oh, so now two of my supposed dates are the problem. Never mind that you were cozy with your pregnant wife that night and I didn't even know about the blind date I'd been set up on until he showed up. And you know what, Dev? Thank fuck he showed up."

"What the hell is that supposed to mean, Vic?"

"Thank fuck he showed up because that strange man showing me kindness was the only reason I made it out of Frederick's with any dignity, and certainly without spilling all my tears and bleeding out my heartaches all over everyone's meals. He saved me from the humiliation of watching you eat out of that bitch's hand. Now, get the hell out of my house and go back to the treacherous whore you married. Have fun figuring out which of your other phone numbers she screwed with. When you don't hear from my brother ever again – you know where to look for answers."

I moved out of the kitchen and went to open the door for him. He reached out to touch me after following me there, but I stepped back. "Do not touch me! Go back home to your wife where you belong. I might have kept us a secret but it was because I didn't want anyone's judgment tearing us apart. That woman set out to destroy her baby daddy's family and then did the same to our relationship. You and your parents can blame me all you want. I'm guilty of far less than either you or your whore of a wife, though. Remember that when you continue to try to shift the blame onto me, asshole!"

I pushed a stunned Devin out the door and slammed it in his face. I threw the locks and then turned and slid down the door. The sob that tore free of my body in an angry, jerky motion was not able to be clawed back. It no longer mattered if Devin heard me breaking over the end of us. It didn't matter if my neighbors bore witness to my heart shattering. Nothing mattered.

Almost nothing mattered. It should have been impossible to break any more than I already was, but his stupid wedding ring glinted at me from across the room. He'd thrown the damn thing weeks ago when I first found out about them and I hadn't seen it since. I'd nearly forgotten about it. If he hadn't worn another ring on his date night, I would have never remembered. The light caught it just right, so that the metal glinted and winked at me tauntingly. Torment, unlike anything else I'd ever known, ripped a horrible keening wail from my bones and there was no one there to hold me together.

No one but the voice on the other side of the door. "Vic, please!" I could hear the pain in his voice, though it didn't register in that moment. I was too lost in my own hurt.

16

DEVIN

VICTORIA SHOVED ME OUT OF HER APARTMENT AND SLAMMED THE door in my face before I could process anything she'd just said. I didn't even understand why I went on the defensive and blamed her for everything - again.

Yes, I did. I was angry after seeing her cry outside of the restaurant earlier. I wanted to know what gave her the right to play the victim when she refused to speak to me, see me, answer the phone, or even respond to a text. Granted, even without all that - had it been true - she deserved to feel everything. Despite trying to put some of the blame at her feet in the heat of the moment, I knew better. She hadn't been alone in her decision making. Hell, I'd gone along with the secret nature of our relationship because I was afraid of losing my best friend - Vic's little brother. I also hadn't wanted to rock the boat with my parents.

All of my introspection left me, along with any hope I had, as a pitiful wailing sob tore through the front door and pierced straight into my heart. I banged on the door in response. "Vic, please!" I begged.

The door never opened. I sat on the other side and listened as my love cried so hard and so long that her voice sounded ragged in the end. She hadn't moved away from the door, and I knew better than to think it was because she wanted me to feel every bit of the grief she expelled. There was no way in hell Vic would want me, or anyone else, to witness her breaking so tragically. That meant shit had really hit her hard, and once again, I felt like the proverbial knife stabbing her in the back.

I had done this. Through my actions, through my unwillingness to bend, and with my accusations that she had somehow harmed us more than I had, there was no doubt that I had broken her beyond repair. At least, I'd broken the part of her who had once been in love with me. After a while, the gut wrenching noises of distress from the other side of the door finally subsided. She never opened it for me. I wasn't even sure if she knew I was still there.

I couldn't imagine adding to her pain any further, so eventually, I stood and left her house.

Something deep down inside me ached because I knew that after the mess I'd just made of things, there was no coming back. I didn't even understand why I felt so compelled to stick up for Justice when I knew what she had been up to. In some warped sense of responsibility to the woman, I made things worse between Vic and me. The evidence of just how calculating Justice had been should have held my tongue, but once again, I hadn't properly processed all that just yet. It wasn't until I had to sit through nearly an hour of Victoria crying herself sick on the other side of her door that I was able to work through some of what had just happened in her apartment.

One thing for sure was that Vic was right. Her biggest crime was that she kept us a secret from everyone. Mine was far bigger, considering I'd married Justice behind Vic's back. I honestly didn't think Justice and I had sex. It felt like a lie the day I woke up with her naked and plastered to my side. Even though I was hung over, seeing her curled up next to me had felt like a lie. The only thing that made me believe I had sex with her had been the fact that there was evidence. My dick had very clearly been somewhere it shouldn't have. It disgusted me to even remember how I had to go to the shower and wash the traces of what I'd done that night off of my body. I couldn't tell Vic about that though. She already knew enough to be shattered by everything I put us through.

No matter what else happened to cause a strain in my relationship with Vic, I had cheated when she had always remained faithful. I had also kept the fact that something happened between Justice and me a secret. I was an asshole for ever throwing the secret nature of our relationship in Vic's face, as if that was the worst problem we had. I was the problem. The shit I did when I was too jealous to handle a situation that Vic had been forced to watch on repeat for more than a year.

I didn't know how to come back from this latest snafu either. After I couldn't get ahold of Vic for a couple days, I went and sat my parents down and explained everything to them. Everything aside from who Justice was carrying on an affair with. That part I kept to myself, and not for the reasons Vic thought. It wasn't about protecting Justice. It was about what I planned to do with that information.

I SPENT the entire trip home stewing over Vic's perspective on things. She was right about everything. What she had done in hiding our relationship paled in comparison to the bullshit I had put her through. It also paled in comparison to the crazy shit my wife pulled.

The same wife who now lived with me because her parents kicked her out when they found out about the surprise marriage and baby on the way. They told her if she was old enough to be married and expecting, she was damn sure adult enough to live with the husband who had knocked her up. She had nowhere else to go. As a result of our idiotic marriage, Justice was, for all intents and purposes, my problem - for now. She turned out to be bigger problem than I could have anticipated though.

Not only had she burned our prenup, stolen money from my safe, but she had blocked and rerouted my calls to and from Victoria. Her crimes had been adding up, and I'm sure she was careful to avoid swiping my phone in range of the cameras, so there was no proof of that shit.

"Hey, where were you?" My fucking fake ass wife called out as I came through the door.

The surprise came when I rounded the corner and noticed that she was wearing next to nothing, having gotten comfortable since we came back from lunch with my parents. My fake girl-friend- turned wife -wore a white, ribbed tank top with no bra and panties that barely covered her anywhere considering they were thongs.

"What the fuck are you doing?" I asked, not in the mood to put up with more bullshit. I hadn't told her where I was off to when I dropped her off so quickly after our lunch, but there was no doubt she knew I went to go hunt down Victoria.

"What do you mean?" The faux innocence seemed out of pocket since she already knew I saw through her bullshit. While it might have once worked on me, there was no going back to her pretend fake nice and easy flirtatious girl next door persona. She was a fucking snake in the grass and not even one that camou-flaged itself well.

The headache that built since I left Vic's place started to throb even harder. It wasn't her being deliberately obtuse with me that caused my head to pound. It was the realization that she'd been this way all along and I had failed to see what was right in front of me in the beginning. My priority had always been Vic. That was where I failed her too. I had glossed over everything else about our situation, including Justice's neediness, while I tried to figure out how to get Vic to bring our relationship into the light. There was no going back with Vic, the secrets, or Justice's bullshit.

"What the fuck are you wearing? You never dress like that around here."

She shrugged. "We've been married long enough, lover. I figured it was time to spice up our relationship, especially since Vic seems to be done with you - finally." She huffed out the last word as her eyes rolled. Like Vic had been the problem all along.

"No."

"What do you mean, no?" Her hands went to her hips, which she jutted out in what was probably supposed to be an enticing gesture. It wasn't.

"You thought I would bring Vic back and you planned for her to see you like this, huh?"

"I don't know what you're talking about." Her voice was clipped, but I could hear the annoyance in her denial. "I wasn't feeling well and wanted to be comfortable. That's all."

"That's odd because you just said you wanted to spice up our married life. Do you even bother to keep track of your own lies?" She shrugged her shoulders and turned her back on me. I didn't miss the fact that she tried to emphasize her ass as she popped it out further before she walked away.

I followed, like an idiot. "Do you want to tell me about how comfortable you got with my phone?" I could see in the way her shoulders stiffened momentarily that she was about to try to lie to me again. She turned to speak and must have noticed the change in my stance because she quickly decided to go with the flow.

Again she shrugged in that, "It doesn't matter," way that made me want to grab her by the hair and throw her out of my house.

Not that I would ever resort to violence with a woman, but damn if it didn't feel at least a little cathartic to imagine it.

"I thought it would be best if you took a break from dealing with her for a while. We have enough going on here with being newlyweds and our baby on the way."

"First of all, that baby isn't mine. The marriage should have never happened. You lied about the baby to trick me into marrying you. I wouldn't be surprised if you set it up to look like we fucked when we never did."

"Oh no, I assure you that really happened. In fact, I bet your little cameras caught the whole sordid *affair*." She emphasized the word affair, and it put me on edge immediately. Especially since I hadn't thought to go back and look at the video evidence from that night. I'm not sure why I remembered the cameras were there when she stole from me, but forgot that I could have checked what I'd gotten up to that night with her. In all likelihood, I'd blocked out the possibility because I didn't want to be guilty of cheating on Vic. If I saw what really happened, it might mean I'd have to face the fact that I had known exactly what I was doing, even if I forgot later.

"Okay, how about the fact that it is NEVER your fucking business to decide who I talk to. I don't care if we're married. I can prove fraud, the fact that we haven't consummated, and get the marriage annulled immediately." There was something else I could prove, but that was a secret for another day and had nothing to do with a possible sex tape I didn't even know I made.

"No, you can't! My parents kicked me out!"

"And how is that my fucking problem?"

"They think this is *your* baby!"

"I guess you'll have to come clean about being a home wrecking whore then, huh? Maybe you should tell them who the baby's dad really is. I'm sure that will put you back in their good graces. Knowing you, you can even spin yourself into a victim roll and royally fuck up Brody's life."

"I've been your fake girlfriend for more than a year. You owe me!" Her demand came out high pitched and full of desperation.

"I don't owe you anything, Justice. You needed a beard, too. We were even on that score. I'm finally beginning to see that you were playing a different game all along, though."

"I wasn't, but I just…. I just… Dammit, Devin, I started falling for you!" She pouted and moved in closer, as if those words mixed with the seductive way she sauntered toward me would be an enticement I couldn't resist.

"Fuck off, Justice. You have sixty days to vacate my property. I was told on the drive home that was all it would take to get an annulment done as well."

"I won't agree to it. I'll tell them that we did sleep together," she rushed the words out in a panic.

"You would be lying in court if you said that."

"They won't know that. Who do you think the court will believe? Your poor, pregnant wife, who you're throwing away for the other woman? You know, since everyone we know is aware that you and I were dating the whole time, but no one knows that it was really Victoria that you were with while I was with Brody. Do you think they'll believe you when we made everyone in our lives fall for our lies about being together?"

"I think that between the DNA test I'm going to request and the fact that I've been recording our conversation," I pointed to the cameras she apparently forgot all about again. "I have a pretty good case to make for fraud, the annulment, and even getting rid of you sooner than 60-days, since you pose a risk to my mental health." I didn't want to slip in the fact that I thought she posed a risk to my life as well, because there was no way I'd give her any ideas.

"You can't record me. That's illegal."

"We're standing in *my* house. I can record whatever the fuck I want in my own house. You don't have to be here." It was my turn to shrug indifferently. "Besides, welcome to the joys of a one-party state. I don't have to get your permission to record."

"I'll go tell Dallas!" She screamed at me.

"I really hope you do. It will save me time in trying to convince Vic to do just that." I also wouldn't admit that Vic would probably never speak to me again after everything I put her through. Justice didn't get to walk away with that satisfaction.

Justice laughed then. "I know her too well. She might have forgiven you for sleeping with me, maybe even marrying me, but she'll never forgive you for continuing to look so damn happy about playing family with me. I think that was one step too far for little miss perfect."

"Oh, I wouldn't hold your breath on that, since she was the one who told me you were playing games and didn't believe that we'd ever really had sex."

"She's just trying to make it seem less awful that you married me and not her."

"Justice, we're done here."

"We're really not." She stomped her foot at me like a petulant child. "I'll go tell your parents you are trying to kick me out. They like me."

"They already know the truth. They were being nice because the baby isn't mine, they know about my plan, and they didn't want to ruin it before I was able to get you out of my life for good."

She spluttered and turned on her heels to leave. "Justice!" I called out. She stopped with her shoulders all the way up to the base of her skull. "Don't think about pulling any bullshit with me or Victoria. You do, and my next move is to go visit your parents with Brody and his wife on the invite list for that conversation."

She huffed and kept a defiant smirk plastered to her face. "There is no you and Victoria. Considering we both know her old ass so well, there never will be again. So, you can try to threaten me all you want, but it won't help you to get her back. That will never happen again." She turned and flounced off to the guest room.

There was no way I could live with the woman, though. Unfortunately, that meant I would have to go through the legal process of getting rid of her - from my house as well as the public perception that we were married.

17

VICTORIA

In the midst of my deepest heartache, I received a random text from my brother, Houston - the oldest of the boys, that I should show up to family dinner and get to know his woman. I rolled my eyes because in my estimation, that was a relationship that was doomed to fail. Truthfully, all marriages and relationships were doomed to be massive shitstorms for anyone who dared to enter into anything more than a fleetingly blessed union.

I probably sounded bitter.

No, I did sound bitter. There was no denying that fact. It had been two weeks since I kicked Devin out of my house and he hadn't tried to contact me again. This time, I knew there was nothing hinky keeping him from reaching out. He simply didn't want to. Last I heard, from Dallas, he still lived with his wife. I supposed he wanted to give it the old college try with her after all. Being an afterthought to the person who broke my heart so completely was part of the bitter party that kept me from being happy for my brother.

That was the plan until someone knocked on my door. When I opened the door, I didn't expect to see Jordan standing there.

"What do you want?" My tone may have been a bit snappy, but I also hadn't heard from Jordan since the manufactured double date incident.

"To apologize. I didn't mean to cause more trouble for you, I swear. When Dallas mentioned that Devin planned to take his wife out for dinner, I thought you needed to see how they behaved together. You needed to see that."

"And the blind dates?"

"That was because he needed to see that you could move on without him too. I'm sorry. All I seem to be doing with your family lately is apologizing for every bad decision I make while trying to guard one of your hearts."

"One of our hearts?" I asked.

"Yeah, you with Devin who refuses to fight the right way for you and Austin and that bitch, Becs."

"What's going on with Austin?"

"You don't know?"

"I saw Becs when my mom forced me on a shopping trip the other day, but we didn't speak." I giggled. "Well, I did call her a home wrecker."

"You did?" Jordan bloomed underneath my admission, as if she had waited for the day one of us would stand up for her.

"I did. It isn't right that my brother thought you were good enough until she forced her way back into his life. I mean, she should have some self respect, since he left her for you how many times?"

Jordan blushed and looked away. "He still keeps going back to her though." Her admission twisted my beat up heart a little more. I couldn't believe my little brother could be so careless with his best friend's heart.

"You mentioned before that my family were all kind of upset with you. Did you ever get that straightened out?"

Jordan's only answer was a quick nod of her head. She refused to meet my eyes, so I decided to give her the chance to make amends with backup. "I'm supposed to go to Mom's house for dinner tonight, so I can get to know Cleo."

"Clea." She corrected.

"Weird name, but whatever." I took Jordan's hand in mine. "Why don't you come along?"

"Who else will be there?"

"Houston didn't say anyone else. Katy and probably Mom and Dad since they live there." We both giggled at that because there was no way my father would ever willingly miss a meal, especially one my mom prepared for him.

"Yeah, okay. That should be fine."

"Of course it is. You're family and always have been, even if Austin lost sight of that when he started thinking with his dick."

"You're not even going to ask what I did to make your family angry with me?"

I shook my head. "We all deserve a little grace, especially when we are trying to navigate a broken heart. I understand that all too well. There's the depression chocolate cake that I dove into head first without hands or utensils, and then there are the unwanted thoughts I've had to work really hard not to follow through with. Trust me when I say, there have been some desperate plans that my poor, pitiful brain cooked up to get Devin back."

"So, why didn't you follow through with any of them?"

"What would be the point? If he wanted me, it should be because he truly wanted to be there with me, not because I tricked him into it with a fake pregnancy or something."

Jordan blushed profusely, and somehow I just knew that was why my family was angry with her, but considering I had thought about the same thing, I understood her desperation. Maybe with her more than myself. Jordan had been in love with my brother for the majority of her life. It was unfortunate that he hadn't returned those feelings. He loved her, but not in the way she wanted him to.

Just as we got into my car to head out to my family's house for dinner, a notification dinged and I opened it without thinking. Stupid me.

Thinking about the day I tied the knot with the love of my life!

The photo was of a finger wearing a wedding band and that finger was attached to the hand that rested on an obvious baby bump. The she-beast-from-hell had even tagged Devin in her little announcement. I growled and threw my phone. Jordan picked it up and took a look before her watery eyes met my own.

"I'm sorry, Vic. You shouldn't have to see that."

I sighed. "It is what it is, I guess. I think you know all about having to watch the man you love fuck off with some woman who doesn't deserve him."

"Then again, maybe they do deserve each other. We're a sad lot, huh?"

"The saddest," I teased despite having to swipe away the few tears that escaped my traitorous tear ducts.

𓆩⸜❤️⸝𓆪

DINNER HAD APPARENTLY STARTED without us. I wasn't offended. It had been ages ago that I managed to make a family dinner, and even though I promised to be there, it was the norm if I wasn't.

"Our oldest grandchild is going to be a boy who can look after any who come after him."

My mother's announcement was a shock to me, especially since I had been her oldest child. It was nice to know how she truly felt about her oldest being a female.

"Like a girl being the oldest would have been a bad thing?" I asked. Instead of coming to stand beside me as I challenged my mom, Jordan remained hidden behind me as all eyes turned in my direction.

My mother gasped, and glared beyond me instead of answering my question. "Victoria Marie, what have you done?"

"What?" My tone was immediately defensive because I didn't understand why she seemed angry with me for showing up to a dinner I was invited to.

"Vic, you should have told me," Jordan said in such a meek voice that I had to do a double take to make sure it was really her speaking.

"Why?" I asked and then glanced around to see more faces in the crowd staring back at us than I had been led to believe would be at this dinner. I hadn't expected Austin or his new woman at all. Still, I knew immediately that her presence was the problem. "You've always been welcome to family dinners. I don't see any need to change that now." I glared directly at Becs, the woman who worked so hard to steal my brother from his best friend, and added: "Not for anyone." Because fuck love. It was a disingenuous beast at best and a disappointing heartbreak at worst. Becs, seated at my family's dinner table, was the embodiment of Jordan's heartbreak. It would be like if my family invited Devin and the she-beast-from-hell to dinner with me.

No one needed their chest cracked wide open. If they didn't want Jordan to show up, then they should have told me that Austin and his new woman would be here. I would have never brought Jordan along with me had I known. Not to spare them, but to spare her heart.

"Vic, I don't know what's going on with you, but this is just making things worse. Why would you put me in this position?"

Well, that made me feel like an ass even though I hadn't known they would be here, she was quick to make herself the victim in the situation.

"I'm sorry. You'll never know how sorry I am that I interfered with things between you." I couldn't believe what I was hearing. Jordan just admitted that she was the one interfering in Austin and Bec's relationship. What the ever loving fuck had I missed?

"Would you like to take a seat?" Mom asked, though I could tell by her tone that she hoped Jordan would decline and just a moment later, she got her wish.

"No. I didn't realize Austin or…" She paused and once again, I felt as though I had missed something major. "I didn't realize they'd be here, or I wouldn't have come. There's been enough trouble from me."

Jordan stormed out after that leaving me there to feel like the ant being fried by a child with a magnifying glass. "What?"

"You knew that Becs would be here tonight." My brother called out to me, accusation deep in each syllable.

"So!" If they wanted to make an enemy out of someone, let them make one out of me. I didn't care that I wasn't aware she would be there. Truthfully, it would make it easier for me to hide away from everyone, to keep my misery to myself. If everyone hated me, that meant no one would come around to see me fall apart.

"So?" My brother mocked my indignant tone.

"So, you decided to be a complete bitch and invite Jordan without telling her we'd be here? You didn't bother to warn me so that my pregnant girlfriend wouldn't be upset?"

"I didn't know you had a girlfriend anymore, pregnant or otherwise," I informed them all.

"You know what I mean. Why would you hurt everyone this way, including Jordan?"

Okay, I was really lost and out of my element, but fuck it. In for a penny and all that. It was time to double down and make sure no one ever wanted to stop by on a whim to witness more than they should of my personal life falling to pieces. "It's not like you care about Jordan anymore."

"I will always care about Jordan. She's been in my life since we were babies. I might not like her very much right now, and she won't ever be close to me again the way we once were, and that's partly my fault for getting too involved when I shouldn't have, but that doesn't mean I want to see her purposely hurt by this family."

Austin was fuming mad with me, but he wasn't even close to done yet. It took everything in me to keep the tears at bay as he continued to tear into me.

"The worst part of what you did, is that you know Becs is pregnant with my baby and stress isn't good for pregnancy. You decided to put her in undo stress anyway all because you're miserable with whatever is going on in your own life and you decided to take it out on everyone else. You might be the oldest, Vic, but you need to grow the fuck up!"

I missed whatever was said between my brother and his pregnant girlfriend as I remembered Jordan telling me that Becs was trying to fake a pregnancy to come between them. I glanced at her stomach and immediately knew Jordan had lied to me. Considering what she had said before running away, I wasn't the only one who she had been lying to.

I caught a glare thrown my way from Becs and decided to double-down again. "Why are you placating the bitch who helped you cheat on your lifelong girlfriend?"

"Jordan has never been my girlfriend and I have never cheated on anyone. Jordan had expectations that didn't align with mine, and if anything, she was the one who constantly tried to sabotage my relationships with Becs. All three times I tried to date Becs before, Jordan did everything in her power to drive her away. The crazy thing is that Jordan didn't try to do it this time. My own fucking sister did instead."

Well, that was news to me and suddenly I felt very bad for Becs.

"She said…" I started to tell them that Jordan had told me a story from the completely opposite perspective with her being the victim, but then she popped back into the room.

"Sorry, I just realized I couldn't leave because Vic brought me here. Victoria, the first time they dated, I was angry because he hadn't said anything to me about our arrangement being over. It felt like he cheated on me, but that wasn't really true, since we were never together that way. The other times, we weren't together either. I just wanted us to be."

"But you said..." I tried to remind her of how she had told me something completely different before. Jordan cut me off before I could finish though.

"No. I'm sorry. I shouldn't have misled you, I just needed someone to hear how I felt, not what was true."

"Are you kidding me?" I lashed out at my friend. "All this time, I thought my brother was doing you wrong and that woman was the one trying to ruin your relationship. Now, you're telling me it was the other way around? I should have known, I guess, since you faked a Goddamn pregnancy to try to trick my brother." That was the other thing I'd forgotten when I showed up with her. My mother had mentioned Jordan's fake pregnancy to me on the phone, but I'd been in the middle of a full mental breakdown and had forgotten all about it until I was faced with my entire family's anger bearing down on me. Damn, go big as an asshole or go home, I guess. Truthfully, I just wanted to go home and wallow, but I was a little miffed with myself for taking everything out on an innocent - I think - pregnant woman.

"Victoria," My dad's admonishing tone hit on the last bit of control I had over my messy emotions. "I think we've all had about enough drama. You brought Jordan here on a night when you knew she wasn't invited, you need to take her home. When you get back, you can apologize for ruining dinner and your brother's announcement."

I turned on my heel and ran from the room with zero intent to come back to my family home. My life had officially fallen all the way apart.

18

VICTORIA

I WAS TRULY ON MY OWN THANKS TO MY INABILITY TO PROCESS ALL the bullshit in my life. My judgement was cracked, and that is the only reason I could find for allowing Jordan to come over and explain everything to me. Supposedly, she told me the truth that time, and it was just ugly enough that I believed her.

I also felt sorry for her. She had been invested in having a happily ever after ending with my brother for longer than I had even known Devin. Part of me understood how big those feelings could be, especially since I'd blocked Dev for real over the past couple weeks and he hadn't even attempted to come see me in person again.

My life consisted of work, home, blubbering into my covers about how sad my existence was and then repeating everything again the next day. If a person could be stuck in a Groundhog Day scenario - it would resemble my life. The only thing that changed were my outfits and the meals that I didn't have the stomach to eat.

I shouldn't be this torn up over a man.

My logical brain knew that. It for sure knew that I shouldn't sabotage my family relationships just to keep my suffering quiet.

That bit of logic was overruled by my feelings too. My parents called to tell me that I wasn't welcome back home until I made a genuine apology to Becs and my brother. While I wanted to do that, I refused. If I did it, there would be questions and those questions would lead to answers I didn't want them to have about my life.

Despite Jordan telling me her whole sad tale, including how my mother invited her to my brothers' wedding, and me understanding, she wasn't even around anymore for me to talk to.

I could have really used a friend around, one who wasn't caught up in her own bullshit, because that meant I hadn't even been invited to their wedding. My parents must have meant business when they said I wasn't invited to come around until I apologized for my behavior toward Becs and Austin. I found it insulting that my mother invited Jordan - the person they were all angry with me for bringing to dinner, but I was a pariah.

It was after that revelation that I called a therapist and scheduled my first visit. I honest to God, could not handle the abandonment from everyone. I knew that part of it was my fault because I had pushed everyone away to keep them from knowing how much I hurt. Still, two of my little brothers got married and I was left out while the woman who caused all the drama between everyone was invited. It felt like a slap in the face. First, Justice stole my future and the love of my life, then my family disowned me because I took Jordan at her word and tried to protect her from the same heartache I suffered.

Life was unfair and I needed help to deal with it.

That was why I decided to crash another one of my family's dinners. No, it wasn't my therapist's idea. She did tell me that I needed to own up to my part of hurting someone else and apologize to Becs, but only if I meant it. Considering I never meant to hurt her, that was an easy ask. I had to remember that my own reasons for doing what I did could stay private, especially since they'd just sound like awful excuses anyway.

ONCE AGAIN, I walked in on a family dinner that started without me. It was like my family completely forgot about me. I looked around and noticed my father wiping some tears free of my mother's face and immediately my hackles went up.

"Proud of you," I heard him mumble to her.

"Why is my mother crying?"

"It's of no matter to you," Mom called out, as if I was no one. I didn't think I had a heart left to injure, but I'd been wrong. Oh, so very wrong.

"Okay, whatever." I guess we were going back to plan A - become the family disappointment and fully commit to pushing them away since they never even missed me or bothered to wonder what had made me so angry, sad, and bitter anyway. It was like no one saw my pain because their lives were all perfect and they didn't want to disrupt the good by dealing with me. Ugh! I was legitimately going crazy as I took my normal seat and then narrowed my eyes at Becs.

Don't do it! Don't do it! Don't do it!

Chanting away the intrusive thoughts didn't work. Nope. Instead, I threw the ugly out at the newest family member. "I hope you're happy with yourself."

"Fuck Vic! What now?" Austin grunted out from across the table as I continued to stare at his girlfriend - wife. Wasn't it lovely that everyone was getting married around me, including my own boyfriend?

"Jordan is moving away, as in out of town. It isn't fair that I couldn't even invite her over for one last family dinner, so she could say goodbye before she leaves tomorrow, all because *she's* here." As far as I knew, Jordan had already left. We hadn't spoken again after she told me everything from the beginning until we were caught up where we left off at the last family dinner I mistakenly brought her to.

"All you had to do was text your brother that she was coming to dinner tonight, and we wouldn't have shown up," Becs tried to be graceful about me going on the attack again, bless her. If only she knew that I was using her as the catalyst to finish blowing up my life. My therapist would be appalled and yet I couldn't stop the vile words from flowing free.

"So, you're just going to hold my brother hostage and not allow him to say goodbye to his life-long friend?"

"As I told everyone at *my wedding*, you know the one you failed to even show up to?" Austin questioned as if I had received an invite. My mother's face turned notably red and I realized that my brothers might not have realized that I hadn't been extended and invitation. "I already said my goodbyes to Jordan. She burned all her bridges with me."

"Because of her," I pointed at Becs while I really wanted to ask my mother why she stopped loving me.

"No," Houston, the oldest of my brothers, stood up and walked around the table to where I sat. "Austin let Jordan go because she could never be honest, and she was always sabotaging his life. Shit, Vic, she tried to bring down our fucking bar, too."

"No, she didn't." Jordan hadn't said a word to me about the bar when we talked.

"Yeah, she did. Ask her about the sexual harassment claim she lobbed against your brother. It wasn't just the drama with the fake baby, or any of the other lies to get Becs away from him over the years. She lied to the authorities about him sexually harassing her and threatening to fire her if she didn't 'perform' for him."

"What?" I asked as my eyes turned back to Austin to see if it was true.

"It happened during the time when we weren't really speaking, but after I learned she faked her pregnancy. We let her go from her job and she tried to make a claim for unemployment, despite getting a severance package. She tried to claim that was hush money."

"Oh, dear Lord," Mom cried from her end of the table. "Why didn't you boys tell us? That makes what I did even worse."

"No, it doesn't." Becs comforted my mother as my father beamed at her for it.

"Why would she do that?" I asked the question, though I hadn't realized I had done so out loud until the answer found me.

"Why did she do any of the bullshit she did?" Austin retorted with his own question. And fair enough.

"The girl was fucking disturbed, and it took unraveling her lies to finally see it because none of us wanted to notice before."

"Hopefully, she gets some fucking therapy wherever she ends up," Dallas chimed in as he filled his plate while everyone else was too busy to complain.

"Vic, I know you want to believe the best in her because you took her under your wing after her mom died, but it's no one's fault she's leaving town. She made that choice on her own, just like she chose to start all the drama she did." Houston sat back down and tucked his wife up in his embrace. Jealousy lit through me, but I knew when to let some things go.

"You all act like Austin's girlfriend-"

"Wife," Austin corrected me without missing a beat.

"Whatever, you act like she's not the real reason."

"That's because she's not, Vic," Houston cut in again. "I don't know why you felt compelled to come throw this fit tonight, but it's not cool. Get your facts and priorities straight before running your damn mouth. One day, you're going to realize life isn't as simple as you try to make it out to be."

Oh, little bro, I already know that. I thought to myself.

"She knows, since she's dating a married man," Katy piped up. I hadn't even noticed she was at the table, and honestly, while I deserved shit to be thrown at me, I didn't expect it to come from my little sister.

"What the fuck?" Dallas snarled as he turned toward me. "Tell me you're not!"

All the color drained from me as I faced my youngest brother and Devin's best friend. Then, I stood and fled my family home once again. I could hear Katy spill my secrets to everyone as I left. It was probably for the best that she didn't know the whole sordid tale.

19

VICTORIA

"Vɪᴄ, ᴡᴀɪᴛ!"

"No!" I shouted back as I climbed into my car and took off. I wasn't near fast enough though because Dallas jumped on his Harley and followed me across town to my place. I parked and ran inside, but he was faster and practically kicked in my door before I could get it shut.

"Stop, Dallas. I don't want to talk about it."

"Tough shit. You've been behaving like a royal bitch, but I didn't see it before."

"See what?"

"The reason," Dallas stated in a quiet voice. "He broke your heart, didn't he?" He did, but I think my brother had drawn a lot of wrong conclusions and that was confirmed by what he said next. "Why would you agree to be his affair partner, Sis? You're better than that."

"I wasn't the affair partner!" I shouted. I dated Devin for more than two years."

"What the fuck?" Dallas asked and then shook his head back and forth in an almost violent manner as I watched him going over memories of the past couple years. "No. He has been dating

Justice for a year and a half. Fuck, they got married, not too long ago. She's having his baby."

"No, she is not having his baby!" I denied emphatically. The longer I went without hearing from Devin, the more I wondered about that though. Maybe he hadn't come back around because he found out it really was his kid. Considering Jordan had lied to me about every-fucking-thing, it was possible that Devin had as well. Maybe the two of them had been fucking around behind my back for the entire time they were fake dating.

"You need to sit down and explain this shit to me." Dallas demanded. So, I did. I broke down and sobbed through every little detail starting with the way Devin chased me when he was still only 19 and I refused to date him because that was cringy. Then, when he had been out of his teens for the better part of a year, I finally agreed to a date. Everything that came after tumbled free from me until I got to today, where I destroyed my brother's poor wife so I could keep everyone away from me.

"Jesus, Vic." My brother grabbed me and pulled me into a hug so tight that it both took my breath and gave me a little hope back. "I'm so sorry you have been going through this. Why didn't you just tell me that you were dating? I wouldn't have cared."

"You did care though. You almost caught us a couple times and we talked about telling you, but then you fussed with Devin about shit. You practically forbade him from dating me."

"That's because he wasn't serious or ready to settle down and have a real relationship with you. I only wanted him to be serious about it if he chose to try to win you - because you aren't a game to be won and then tossed aside when the challenge is over. You're my big sister, but I can still look out for you. Obviously, he still wasn't ready to do right by you or he never would have agreed to keep things secret. He sure as fuck would have never pretended to date another woman, let alone fuck her so she could try to baby trap him. He should have never agreed to marry the conniving bitch if he was so damn ready to settle down with you."

"Thanks for the heart-wrenching recap of the recap of my shitty fucking existence, Dallas." I rolled my eyes and wiped my snotty nose on his shirt.

"Gross, Vic." He glanced down and made a disgusted face before he shrugged it off and pulled me back in for another hug. "I wish you would have come to me sooner. WAY FUCKING SOONER. I can't believe you tried to piss everyone off to keep them all away while you went through hell on your own."

"I wasn't totally alone. I had Jordan for part of it."

"Yeah? How'd that work out for you?"

"I still can't believe she lied to me about everything. She was family. I feel like no one can be trusted, myself included."

"Sounds to me like you need some serious therapy."

"Already started and she's going to be so upset with me when she finds out what I did." I sighed. "Honest to God, I went there to apologize to Becs tonight and…" I cried into my baby brother's chest some more. "I don't know what happened. Mom was… Well, she sounded like she didn't want me there. I was never invited to Houston and Austin's wedding, Dallas. You have to believe me."

"I do. I saw Mom's face when Houston mentioned it. She never told you, even though she was the one who was supposed to notify everyone since it was last minute."

I nodded. "She hates me. My own mother hates me. How can I expect Devin, or any other man, to love me when I'm not even lovable to my own mother?"

"Shut your mouth, Vic. You are. Mom fucked up. Hell she fucked up so bad she disinvited you and brought Jordan along to the wedding."

"Yeah, that's even more of an insult, considering Jordan's lies are why I had the outburst to begin with. How is it possible for Mom to forgive her and not me?"

"She didn't forgive her. Mom brought Jordan there to see Austin getting married so she would give up on him and go find her own peace."

"That sounds a lot like forgiveness when you want the other person to be happy."

"Maybe so, but I don't think Mom hates you. Everyone is under a lot of stress and there are things we don't all know about, obviously." My brother glanced down to give me a very pointed look. "Just for the record, I am going to kill Dev, though."

"No. You're going to pretend like you know nothing."

"Nah, fuck that. He fucked with my big sister and broke her in a way I never thought I'd see in my lifetime. That fucker lied to me, for years, and still had the nerve to call me his best friend."

"He did it for me."

Dallas shook his head. "No, he didn't. He might have said so. He might even have lied to himself that it was for you, but he did it for himself too. His parents wanted him to settle down with a girl from his office a couple years ago. Well, his mom did. His dad thought he was too young to settle for anyone. Both of them have tried to dissuade him from the crush he had on you for years."

I huffed and shrugged out of my brother's hold then. "Well, that's a pleasant thought."

"I don't think they did that because they don't like you. They did it because it didn't seem plausible and they wanted him to live his life instead of being sunk neck deep inside a crush that went on for way too long. I told him the same fucking thing many times, granted a few of them were while you two were dating secretly." Dallas gave me a knowing look that was meant to make me feel guilty. It kind of did, because my life would have been far less complicated if only we'd just been honest with everyone upfront.

"If I thought you were interested in him, I never would have tried to push him to date other people."

"I know that."

"All right. Good talk." My brother said as he walked to the door. "No more secrets. They're not good for our family."

"Take your own advice then!" I shouted back as he closed the door after he walked out. I ran after him. When I got the door opened, I yelled to my brother as he put his helmet back on. "Where are you going?" I wanted to add, 'so abruptly,' but that was a given.

"I have a nose to break, big sis. Go back inside and lock up. If you need me, call, but not for the next hour or so."

I didn't even bother to beg him not to break Devin's nose. My ex deserved a little pain for everything he put me through.

20

DEVIN

"GO TO HELL, YOU BASTARD!"

I chuckled as my *wife* left the house angry with me once again. It was the only joy I had in life anymore. Vic blocked me weeks ago, so I couldn't call or text to check on her. Once in a while, I would drive by her place to see if she would notice, but she never did. Her house was always dark, though, so it was hard to tell.

I wanted to go to her. To be with her. To promise her that she is my everything and the only future that could possibly make me happy. I couldn't though. Not yet.

Our time was coming and I had just set off step one in getting Victoria Mercer back in my life. More than that, I wanted to be in her heart again the way she still was in mine. Unfortunately, I had some legal hoops to wade through first, and then we would be able to have the future we always hoped would be possible.

My parents were finally on board, but then again, I wasn't sure they had a whole lot of faith that I could win my girl back. Truthfully, depending on the day, my own hope wavered, especially the longer I went without being able to talk to her. I knew there was no way we could try again, so long as Justice was still in the picture. That was priority number one. I had Justice served with a 60-day notice to vacate my property. She defiantly said she would fight it because we were married and even if I had video to prove that there was a prenup, I didn't have any proof of what was in it. So, technically the house was marital property and we lived in a no-fault state.

If I thought it would get me free of her quicker, I would sign the fucking house over to her. Not that I wanted to. I owned the thing free and clear, thanks to money my grandfather left me when he died. Still, my lawyer told me to hold off as long as possible and play the long game because grifters didn't deserve a piece of the pie. He wasn't wrong about that. Besides, I didn't want her to be rewarded for coming between Vic and me.

"Are you sure you don't want to press charges against her for sexual assault? It was clear from your security footage that you were extremely intoxicated when things happened between you."

I shook my head and cringed as my lawyer laid it out for me. "No." It took me a while to find the moment in the video where I lost faith in my relationship with Vic and stepped out on her. I did that, even if I didn't remember afterward. "I've seen rape cases where women were just as messed up and they couldn't win. I won't file charges under the same circumstances and hope for better. I'm not sure why I can't remember the evening, but I was speaking clearly for the most part when it happened."

"I wouldn't say you spoke clearly. You called out another woman's name repeatedly and it was slurred so bad it was almost incomprehensible." My lawyer offered and if we weren't on the phone, I'd bet money his eyes rolled. "You didn't even know who you were with that night, Devin."

"I don't want to press charges unless it is a last resort measure."

"Fine. I'm keeping the video just in case. It will remain secured and still falls under attorney-client privilege even if you choose not to use it to your advantage."

"Great." Someone banged on my door and I swore under my breath as I got ready to hang up with my lawyer.

"One more thing, Devin. We're double checking the surrounding counties, just in case she took it upon herself to go file the certificate. My investigator was not able to find any public record of your marriage."

"That means no one ever filed it, right?"

"We'll check in with the idiot who runs the quickie wedding spot you used, but it doesn't look like it. Besides, the certificate you gave me looks to be the original one without the state seal on it."

"That's good news, so now the only complication I might run into is if she claimed squatters rights."

"That's it. Good job on not filing that certificate. You made things a lot easier on yourself."

I scoffed. "I don't know about that." Someone banged on my front door again. "Gotta go, someone is here and they are relentlessly banging my door down."

"Let me know if you need anything else and I'll be in touch with any updates as they come in."

I grunted my acknowledgement as I hung up and moved to the front door. No sooner did I open it than a fist flew into my face and knocked me straight on my ass.

"You fucking piece of shit! You broke my sister!"

"I'm trying to fix everything!" I cried out, though it sounded garbled since my nose had already started to swell and blood dripped down into my mouth. "Broke my fuckin' nose."

"You deserve worse," Dallas huffed at me.

"I know," I agreed. "How is she?"

"How the fuck do you think?"

"I haven't seen her and she blocked my phone a couple weeks ago." It sucked to admit that to my best friend, but especially because he was also her brother.

"Good for Vic. She knows her worth." He sighed and shut the

door then slid to the floor beside me. "Sort of," he added at the last minute.

"What does that mean?" The bastard winced and shook his hand out as I watched through watery eyes.

"Come on," Dallas huffed as he got back to his feet and held his left hand out to help me up. His right looked a bit swollen and I felt the tiniest amount of satisfaction that the sucker punch he'd thrown at my face hurt him too. "Let's talk in the kitchen while I get some ice for this." He held out his sore hand as he said that.

"What about this?" I pointed to my face.

"Live with it the same way my sister has been living with a broken heart all by herself."

"What do you mean all by herself?"

"She has literally no one, asshole." I stopped mid-stride as he said that.

"What about Jordan?"

I reluctantly had to follow behind Dallas as he continued to my kitchen on a mission. "Jordan is out of the picture and last I heard out of state by now too."

"What the fuck happened?"

Dallas shrugged his shoulders and then slowly recounted everything that had been going on in Austin's life and how that affected Vic too, since she used it - and what she believed to be the truth - to push her family away.

"At this point, I don't know why she's still keeping our relationship a secret."

"Well, for two reasons, asshat. The first being you no longer have a relationship. As far as my sister is concerned, you chose your wife. The second being that she's embarrassed to have been thrown away for the devil bitch. You're still living with the woman, dipshit."

That was when I sat my best friend down and told him the plan to rid myself of Justice once and for all. I hoped that it was also the plan to win Vic back, but time would tell.

"Man, I wish I was going to be here to see that shit play out."

"Where are you going?"

"I'm headed out for the holidays on my own private getaway. My family is too fucking much these days."

"Did you ever tell them about what you really do for a living?"

He grinned at me. "Besides co-own the Tippler's Lounge with my brothers?" He asked.

"Yeah. They had to wonder where you got the investment funds."

Dallas shrugged. "Funny thing about being me, no one ever asked where I got the money. I didn't offer up any details either."

"Secrets have a way of festering before they come to light," I reminded him.

"Yeah, well they're going to fester while I soak up some sun on a tropical beach for a couple weeks." He managed to get some ice into a ziplock bag and then dropped it down over his knuckles while we talked. I grabbed a bag of frozen peas to put on my face.

"Not going to forget that you lied to me for two years," Dallas stated as he moved to head back to my front door.

"Yeah? Keep that grudge in mind when your family finds out you're a fucking billionaire and didn't tell them."

"I hope your nose hurts!" Dallas offered as he left my house and went back out to his motorcycle.

"Can you drive that thing with a busted up hand?" I called out to him.

"Fuck you. Fix my sister, asshole!" He revved his engine loudly, so he couldn't hear my nonexistent response. A moment later, he was gone and I returned to my house to execute the next step in my plan. I had to upload a very personal article to the local newspaper.

21

VICTORIA

AFTER I CONFESSED EVERYTHING TO MY BABY BROTHER, HE LEFT town. No one in the family knew where he went, and it worried them all enough that I started to get phone calls.

It made sense, I guessed, since the last time they saw him, he had gone charging off after me to find out what was going on between his best friend and me. I couldn't help but think he had done this disappearing act on purpose, though.

After the third text from a family member inquiring about Dallas, I finally called my dad and had him set up a family meeting. Thankfully, Dallas reached out to let me know where he was and that he'd be back once the family wasn't acting like a bunch of "shitheads" to one another. His word, not mine.

I wasn't sure if that was something I planned to say to my family or not, but either way, they deserved an apology from me - for real this time. They also deserved the truth of what was going on in my life. If no one wanted to talk to me after they knew the truth, then I would have to live with that.

MY FAMILY, all of them minus Dallas, stared at me somewhat slack-jawed for far too long after I explained everything that had been going on.

"I don't understand why you would ever think we cared who you loved." My dad told me.

"Oh, I care. That fucker has a lot to answer for," Houston finally popped off.

Austin remained quiet and held onto his wife's hand. I had apologized profusely to the both of them, but my apologies were met with cold indifference. Even after I explained why I had gone off the deep end, they remained frigidly indifferent. I didn't blame either of them for their response - or lack of one. I deserved far less than they were giving.

"I have it on good authority that Dallas already broke Devin's nose and gave him two stunning black eyes," I mentioned.

My mom harrumphed at that. "Violence is never the answer."

"Agree to disagree," my father blurted out.

"What Dad said," Houston chipped in.

My heart ached from being so close to my family while not feeling fully a part of them. I wouldn't push for more than I had given over the past year and a half though. They all deserved better from me and I couldn't expect to get more back from them, though I was surprised that Houston seemed to have my back in this.

"You know," Mom said as she stood from the circle of chairs we all occupied. "This does at least explain the article. At first, I thought he was talking about that awful girl, but I see now that he was talking about you."

"What are you talking about, Mom?"

She grinned and left the room in search of whatever it was. While she was gone, Houston came over and gave me a hug. "I know that was hard for you, but I wish you had trusted us with all this a lot sooner. It might have made things easier on your relationship."

"It definitely would have kept Justice from having room to push into your relationship," My brother's wife added. I still didn't know Clea well - or at all, really. I nodded to her, though.

"You're all probably right, but there isn't anything I can do to change what has already taken place."

We sat silently for a bit and waited for Mom to come back. "Finally!" Mom declared as she came back around the corner carrying her tablet with her. "Sorry I took so long, I had to find the article again. It was on the socials this morning, but I couldn't remember what the title was. I had to try to find it on the Googles instead."

I wanted to laugh at my mother, but managed to refrain as she shoved the tablet in my direction. I took it with shaking hands and started to read the article she had pulled up.

The Decision that Ruined my Life.

Devin's name was just below the title in the byline.

I skimmed through the article and it was mostly the beginning of our relationship and how we never should have hidden what we had from anyone because their opinions never mattered to our happiness anyway. At the end, there was a reminder this was only part one of a four-part series in finding and losing the love of his life.

When I was done reading, I glanced back up at my mom who sat there with tears in her eyes.

"I cried when I read that this morning. I cried for Devin and the woman who he obviously loved with all his heart. I didn't know then that he was talking about my oldest daughter. I don't understand why you wanted to hide that from us."

"The way he described loving you," Clea stated, as she held her hand over her chest. She passed her phone to Becs who started reading the article too. "Are you sure it can't be fixed?"

"I guess you'll have to wait for the other parts of his series to come out to find out why. As far as I know, he's still living with her, still married to her." I shrugged my shoulders and then stood up. "Look, I came to offer my sincere apologies, let you know not to worry about Dallas, and..."

"And nothing. Sit your boney ass down and get ready to eat some food. You look like you've been starving and you will not allow any man to take your figure away from you!" My mother gave her marching orders before she ran off to the kitchen. When I tried to stand and leave anyway, my eyes connected with my father's. He shook his head and pointedly looked at the seat I had just vacated.

"Don't even think about it," He all but whispered to me.

Well damn. I guess I had to stick around for a few awkward rounds of: "Let's dissect your shitty life".

"I'm sorry too, Vic. I shouldn't have said anything, but you made me so mad when you were being hateful to Becs for no reason." Katy huffed and her pouty lips looked even more prominent on her face as she brooded over my behavior. "And that was after you refused to go to Houston and Austin's wedding."

I wasn't about to throw our mom under the bus, so I simply nodded like it was the truth.

"No!" I heard Mom yell as she quickly scooted back into the room and pointed her wooden spoon at me. "I will not have you sit silent on another thing. It was not your sister's fault that she missed the wedding."

"What do you mean?" Houston asked.

"I never invited her." My mom admitted with her head hung low in shame.

There was a collective gasp throughout the room as everyone's attention shifted from my mom to me, as if searching for me to deny her truth or validate it. I gave the slightest of nods to indicate it was the truth and nothing else.

"Why, Mom?" Houston asked her. "None of us will ever get those moments back. Two of her brothers got married and she wasn't even invited." My brother's eyes swung back to me and I could see the damage that had been done. "I accused you... That night..." He paused again to search for his words. "No wonder you were so angry with everyone. We were all so wrapped up in our own shit that no one ever bothered to check on you and then you found out that we had a double wedding and you didn't even get invited." He shook his head. "I'm so sorry, sis. That invite should have come directly from me."

"Don't worry about it. It's all in the past now."

"Obviously not," Houston said as he glanced between all of our siblings who were present and then back at Dad whose furrowed brow indicated that he hadn't known about Mom snubbing me either.

"So, I'm going to therapy." I threw the admission out there to break the ice, but all it did was make my mother cry her way back into the kitchen. For a few minutes, she was left there alone until my father stood and came over to put a warm hand on my shoulder.

"I'm so sorry, kiddo." He let go and went into the kitchen before I could say anything.

"I feel like I caused even more drama and I wasn't even trying this time," I half-ass joked. "I'm going to..." I stood and hitched a thumb toward the door.

"Please, stay," Houston pleaded.

"No offense, but part of therapy is knowing my own limits and I'm just about at the end of what I can handle for one day."

"Can I come with you?" I turned to see Katy hovering there nervously, and gave her a quick nod. "I'll go grab a bag. Don't leave without me."

If nothing else, being honest with my family, and reading what Devin had to say about the beginning of our secret relationship, did one good thing. It brought me back into the fold of my family. We weren't perfect - far from it, but as my therapist was known to say: Now that the truth is free, the healing can start.

22

DEVIN

I HOPED LIKE HELL VICTORIA HAD BEEN READING THE ARTICLES I'D been posting to the lifestyles and entertainment section of our local newspaper. It took a rather large donation to get the editor to agree to it in the first place and then he only agreed to the subsequent posts because of how popular the first one was. As if humbling myself to the woman I loved more than anything wasn't hard enough. The damn ode to our broken relationship had received national attention.

At first, everyone thought that I was talking about my love affair I supposedly had with Justice. Things obviously weren't adding up though, as was evidenced by the comment section on each post. So, then everyone tried to figure out who in the hell had stolen my heart so much that I was making very public posts about loving a woman who wasn't my wife.

I wondered if it would all backfire on me because Victoria had always been big on privacy. She was the one who initially wanted us to remain a secret. It was possible that telling our story would make her dig further into hiding away. Then again, she and her family had been seen spending more time together, so I assumed the relationships there had been healed. They were at least better than they were when Dallas took off for his vacation and then never came back.

That too sat like a heavy weight on my shoulders, because I felt like I was part of the reason my best friend had been driven away from our town. I knew the way his family saw him - as a full-grown man-child who refused to grow up - had always bothered him, but not enough to stop being true to himself. If they only knew he was the most successful person in our whole town, let alone their family.

I glanced around nervously once more and tugged on my tie as I stood off to the side of the stage at the Tippler's Lounge. Houston knew what I was about to do and had approved it. I wish he wasn't the first to know. That honor should have gone to Victoria. Since it was the Mercer brothers' bar, I needed someone's permission. We also needed to coordinate for extra security for the revelations that were coming down the pipeline instead of resolutions.

It was New Year's Eve and I hated that I hadn't been able to spend Christmas with my woman, but my lawyer and I finally had all our ducks in a row and it was time to give the love of my life, and the rest of the town, a little insight into the final article I had to publish in my series on Monday.

Depending on how it all worked out, it might be a happy ending to some, or a beautiful beginning for Vic and me. Then again, it all might go to shit and it would just become a cautionary tale for the masses. Secrets never remained and life was too short for them anyway.

I scanned the crowd once more and was annoyed to see that Justice was there. It sickened me to watch as she laughed with Melissa, Brody's wife, while he stood by and allowed that interaction. I supposed he had to. What was he going to say? *'Don't talk to our best friends' daughter because I've been sleeping with her for the better part of two years and that baby she is carrying is mine.'*

I didn't think it would work out well for him, but then again, everyone's secrets were going to be spilled by the end of the night anyway. It would probably be better for him if he did come out and say it. I wondered if the new apartment Brody was paying for, to house his mistress and their soon-to-be-born son, would become their home together after this. Not my circus.

My eyes trailed over the crowd until I finally saw her. My beautiful Victoria wore a black beaded dress with thin straps. It came up just above her knees and depending on the lights she walked under, her dress looked as though it was embellished with silver, then gold, then a red hue. The lights caught and reflected the beading just right to give her an ever-changing appearance that suited her vivacious personality.

The very same personality that had been dulled and refused to shine for months - since she found out I had fucked us up with my jealous tantrum. It was good to see her wearing something that suited the confident woman she was supposed to be. Her red lips stood out almost as much as the dress did. Vic always had beautiful, full lips that made you want to linger and suck at them for days. The red lipstick she wore on them seemed like a beacon meant to draw me close and do just that.

Her blonde hair was left loose with a bit of a wave to it and it swayed and shimmered under the lights with every step she took. I wasn't sure if it was a statement, or simply went with the dress, but she wore the platinum and diamond necklace I bought her for our second dating anniversary. The little bit that dangled from the column of her throat seemed to point straight down the cleavage she had on display.

"You going up there or what?" I turned my attention away from Vic to find her brother standing there beside me. Austin glanced down at his watch and then back up at me. "Houston said you were supposed to go up and give some speech before the big ball drop. That's less than ten minutes away, so you're running out of time."

"I think everyone will forgive me."

Austin tried to stifle his chuckle, but failed. "Something tells me you only need one particular person's forgiveness."

"You're not wrong." I called back to him as I hopped up on the stage and made my way to the microphone positioned front and center.

I adjusted my tie for the fiftieth time that night and smoothed down my tailored black suit pants. Everyone was dressed to the nines for the New Years' Eve bash, and I was no exception. I wanted to wear something that matched with Vic, on the off chance I ended the night with her back in my arms. It seemed fitting that we should be able to make a public debut while looking our finest. Still, no one would tell me what she planned to wear, so I had gone with solid black from head to toe and was thankful for it because we ended up matching perfectly.

"Can I get everyone's attention?" I called out. Vic was the first head to turn in my direction. That might not have been true, but hers was the only one I noticed. "For those of you who don't know who I am, I'm the sad sap who has been writing the articles in the local paper about how I ruined my relationship with the best woman to ever walk the planet."

Vic's lips tipped up at the corners even though she tried to hide her reaction. Other people turned in her direction too, having noted who had all of my attention.

"The woman I have been talking about in those articles deserves a far better man than me, but I'm hoping she will reconsider dating beneath her station after she hears what I have to say tonight."

Vic lifted a brow, as if to say: "I'm listening." So I decided not to keep her in suspense. "I love you, baby. I have always loved you, but I fell so much harder than I ever thought possible. The last few months have been absolutely miserable without you. The last year and a half has been a mixed bag of fake relationships to hide what we had and the blissful days where it was just the two of us. I want that back. The me and you part, but out in the open because we both deserve to be seen and so does the love we share.

"I know I hurt you, we hurt each other because we were too busy trying to live up to what other people thought we should be. Who they thought we should be with." I tacked on the last because it was true. When my parents first found out I was dating Justice, they had been happy to know that I was finally over my obsession with Dallas's big sister. Little did they know then that it was all a ruse.

"I laid everything out in the article I wrote, but the part I didn't spill yet is that my love wanted to hide our relationship from all of you because she feared your judgment. She was afraid of what you would think about her dating a younger man - her littlest brother's best friend."

Gasps and other sounds of shock and surprise rose up amongst the crowd as Vic slowly made her way closer to the stage. I wondered if she moved closer in an effort to get me to shut up. Then I looked down and saw the smile on her face and knew that wasn't it. She was onboard for whatever was about to go down.

"We went so far as to bring a third person into our relationship - though not our bed. Get your minds out of the gutter," I teased. "The girl we chose for me to 'fake date' needed a fake boyfriend too. I'm not proud of my involvement in what she was doing, but I'm about to lay it all on the line for you."

I pointed out into the audience, close to the bar, where Justice huddled in near her parents and Brody looked like he had seen a ghost. His head shook back and forth as if he could get me to stop this train before I derailed his life. No such luck, buddy. He had no problem allowing me to take the blame for his baby momma drama, so I had no qualms about the next words that came out of my mouth.

"I need you all to know that Justice was only ever a fake girlfriend and only in public. She needed a fake boyfriend to hide the affair she was having with her dad's best friend, Brody. That is his baby in her belly. Well, I can't say that for sure, but that is what she told me. They've been seeing one another for the better part of a year and a half, almost two years now. In fact, Brody just leased an apartment for his growing little family to live in."

We all heard the shriek from his wife just as Justice's dad laid his best friend out with a single punch. "Nice job!" I called out. "And by the way, your daughter is crazy and tried to blackmail me. Nasty business there. I have it all on video, as well as her admitting to breaking into my safe, setting fire to legal documents, stealing a felonious amount of money, and some other potential crimes I don't think should be mentioned here. We'll just say I don't remember the night she claimed I got her pregnant. The same night that led to me marrying her."

More gasps rang out around the room and that was when my attention moved back to Vic who had stopped a few feet short of the stage. "There is another revelation we can be thankful for. Justice and I were never actually married."

"Yes, we were!" Justice yelled.

"No, we pretended to get married, just like we pretended to date. The papers were never filed - kind of like that prenup you set fire to." I winked at her and the taunt did its job as she shrieked in response. Her parents turned their backs on her and walked away just as Austin stopped Brody's wife from slugging Justice.

I wished he wouldn't have because she deserved that hit, but I understood that he couldn't let a heavily pregnant woman be abused in his club, even if the bitch did deserve it.

"Victoria Marie Mercer," I called out into the microphone. "Would you do me the honor of being my first kiss of the New Year and the last woman I kiss in this lifetime?"

Vic was there as I jumped off the stage. I pulled her into my body and held her face between the palms of my hands as I leaned in and counted down the final seconds to midnight.

"This is our year, baby. We get to live it any way we want and forget about what everyone else thinks."

"Okay," she whispered against my lips as everyone shouted out the final seconds of the countdown. "THREE, TWO, ONE! Happy New Year!" My mouth dropped onto hers and we rang in the New Year with a fresh slate, the secrets behind us, and a sizzling kiss for everyone to witness.

"I missed you," she whispered against my ear after I pulled away.

"You've been in my heart this whole time, baby. It's you and me and fuck the world."

That made her giggle. "I like that."

"Good because that's our new motto moving forward." She nodded just as flashes from cameras started to go off around us. "I hope you're okay with the limelight for a while, my last article went live on the website a few seconds ago and it reached a national readership."

"I think I can handle it if you're by my side."

"I'm not going anywhere ever again, Vic. I promise."

I pulled the microphone back up to my lips and spoke to the crowd one more time, but I did it after dropping to my knees in front of the woman I loved. This bit, this promise of our future, was worth begging her for.

"Hopefully, one day we can sit in our rocking chairs on the porch of the house where we raised our family, and look back at this crazy time in our lives and laugh it off as our disastrous beginning. The rocky start won't matter by then, only the rest of our story that we decide to write together. I love you Victoria, and I am begging you in front of all these people to give me another chance. A better chance to love you the way we both deserve to be loved."

"I'd love that," She said loud enough for the microphone to pick up. Everyone cheered for us and it was the best feeling after the years of worrying what everyone would think about our age difference. The distance between our years never mattered to me before. What always mattered was how much I loved the woman she was and how well she loved me back.

EPILOGUE

VICTORIA - 22 YEARS LATER

THE HORIZON WAS PAINTED IN PURPLES THAT FADED TO PINK AND then red. It had to be the prettiest sunrise I'd ever seen. I sat there in my wooden white rocker and watched as the morning light slowly dimmed the shine of those colors only to make way for orange and golden hues to take center stage.

"Gorgeous!" I turned to see my husband walk toward me and I smiled at him.

"You should have seen it a few minutes ago. The colors were so different."

"I wasn't talking about the sky, baby. All of those colors pale in comparison to you." I rolled my eyes at the cheesy line my husband threw at me. For some reason, it reminded me of that crazy New Year's Eve when he declared his love for me in front of everyone. It made me grin to think back on that moment, when he humbled himself on his knees before me and talked about a moment much like this.

"What's that smile for?"

"Do you remember that New Years' Eve?"

"The one when you agreed to finally be mine forever?" He asked and I nodded. "Of course, I do."

I patted the rocking chair next to mine and he came to take a seat beside me. "Well, your vision of the future is finally here. It only took twenty-two years, but here we are, on our rocking chairs, staring at the sunrise, and remembering all those years of loving one another."

"She's a romantic today!" Devin declared to the sky and followed it up with a hoot and laughter as he took my hand in his. "I had another vision of our future."

"You did?"

"Yup, a few years from now, we'll be rockin' our grand babies together."

"Stop it! Jessie just graduated high school." I mentioned as a wave of sadness hit me at the prospect of being empty nesters too soon for my liking.

"Maybe so, but Josh already has two years of college under his belt."

"Hmm," I mumbled as I thought back to the day Devin first made me a promise about sitting on our porch and reminiscing in our rocking chairs. "Little did we know that Josh would come into our lives so soon." I giggled.

"Seems to me fate was at play when you weren't able to go get that shot, baby."

That was true enough. I wouldn't ever wish to relive the heartache of thinking the love of my life was building a family with someone else. Devin had a point though. It was precisely that moment in time that set the stage for Josh to come along the following October. It happened after we officially got back together as a couple who were no longer interested in hiding their relationship. I had never gone back for my birth control shot, and we didn't bother with condoms during our makeup marathon sex that lasted the rest of the holiday break. Three days, and four wild nights together before we went back to work, amounted to a brand new start and a little bundle of joy on the way shortly thereafter.

I never regretted the way our lives spiraled ahead at full steam. It felt natural, and we learned some solid lessons during that time that served us well throughout the rough patches that inevitably happen in every marriage. When all was said and done, Devin was still my person. I was still his. And now that our youngest child was off to college too, we had plans to go explore the world together.

"You ready to go rekindle that old flame in Italy?" My husband asked, as if he had just read my mind.

"I'm ready for everything with you."

"You better be, we already got our happy ending, now the rest is just the cherry on top, baby."

I rolled my eyes at the way he laid the cheese on extra thick. "I love you, Dev."

"Always have and always will, Vic."

MORE TO COME IN LOVED FOR THE HOLIDAYS

If you already read:

- Cupid Broke my Heart

- Ghosted by Texas

- Resolving Rumors

Don't worry, there is more to come from the Loved for the Holidays Series by Anne Storm.

Going Out With a Bang is Katy's story. She is the youngest Mercer sibling and her holiday book will involve an important event on the Fourth of July.

Saving Santa is Dallas's story and will obviously revolve around Christmas. It will be available in December 2025.

CHECK OUT MORE FROM ANNE STORM

The Homewrecker's Fate

Cheating Hearts Series #1
Anne Storm

Chapter 1

February 14th

Champagne glasses tipped on their sides spilling the 300-dollar bottle of Ace of Spades Champagne Gold onto the hardwood floor beside the plethora of blankets Rich had thrown down when he made our little love nest in front of the fire. There was only a brief moment to mourn the loss before he rolled me so that I was completely laid out beneath his beautifully sculpted body.

"I'm so in love with you." Those murmured words were burned into the sensitive skin just below my ear as Rich placed a kiss there. Then, he relaxed back just enough that our eyes could meet. "You have changed my life, Aviva Acker. One day soon, we'll be able to be together without always feeling the impending doom every time I have to pack up and go home."

"I don't know why you pack up. You could leave things here," I whispered. Our eyes locked once more as the smile stretched across his face. His large hands cupped my cheeks as his thumbs slid back and forth across my jawline on one side and my lips on the other.

"I'll do that," he reassured me. "Does this mean you're going to give me a key?"

"Well, I'm not trying to hold your belongings hostage." He leaned in and kissed the words from my lips. It left me breathless as he rocked his body against mine, reminding me that we were very naked and discussions about moving in might kill the mood. "I'll leave it on the dresser for you in the morning."

"What did I ever do to deserve you?"

"You have treated me like your precious princess since the moment we met."

"Oh, was that all I had to do?"

A wicked grin lit my face as I shook my head and grabbed hold of his silky, hard length. "Well, there's also the fact that you give the absolute best orgasms."

He chuckled at my admission. "I do believe you were ready for number three before I ruined things with the serious talk."

I swatted his ass with my other hand. "You could never ruin anything by telling me that you love me."

"Well, in that case," Rich shifted his hips so that his cock fell out of my grip and lined itself up with my entrance, almost like magic. Then again, over the past five months, we had worked exceptionally hard at learning one another's bodies. There was no doubting he was an expert in how to handle mine or his own for that matter. A long and low desperate moan tore from me as my love thrust into my body at a languid pace. He kept things slow and steady until the entirety of his length was sheathed within me.

"Rich," I groaned as he bottomed out and the tip of his cock nudged my cervix. The first time he bumped my cervix was always met with a swift punch of pain until my hormones took over as his thrusts increased. Only then did that tiny bite of pain eventually give way to some of the most explosive orgasms I have ever had in my entire 31-year existence.

"I am so fucking in love with you," Rich cried out as he swirled his hips and then slammed back into me.

"Ahhh!" I groaned as the pinch of pain hit once more. From experience, I knew it wouldn't be much longer until everything tipped to sheer pleasure, but I had never been able to hold back the noises he elicited from me.

"I love you." The words were a whimper against his chest as I nipped at the flesh there. His cock slid back out of me only to slam home again while he clenched his muscular arms around my upper body, locking me in tighter, exactly where he wanted me. Despite him having my arms trapped at my sides, I still had a little power in the position. I flattened my feet to the blankets beneath us and lifted my pelvis, tilting it just enough that when he slammed home again, he went even deeper. That did it. The balance tipped from nips of pain to overwhelming pleasure.

"God, yes, Avi! Never had it this fucking good before." His hips worked faster, pumping harder into me as I lifted to meet each thrust and clamped down on my muscles at the same time. The clench made him lose his mind. "Fucking hell! The way you move your body and take all of me... You are a fucking goddess."

I would have giggled at that proclamation, but it was impossible as his rougher thrusts finally triggered another climax. My toes curled, nose went numb and tickly the way it usually did, and then I was lost to a completely different sensation as pain and pleasure melded into pure bliss. Warm tingles and the deepest contentment and peace flowed through me as I floated somewhere outside of my own body for just a moment in time.

All too soon, I was pulled back by the grunts of the man above me and the erratic thrusting that signaled Rich was about to find his release, too. Warm jets of cum splashed my insides as he throbbed within me. One of these days, if we weren't careful…

I trailed my fingers languidly down his sweat-slicked back as he finally rode out the last waves of his orgasm and slowly came back to me.

"We forgot again," I reminded him. "Unless you don't mind having little demigods with me, we should probably be more careful."

He chuckled while sliding out of me before rolling to his side and pulling me with him. "While I would love nothing more than to have babies with you, we should probably be living in the same place before that happens. Have you thought any more about transferring to my office?"

"You know why I can't." My fingers traced a path between each of his nipples, playing there in the crisp chest hairs that gathered in that space between his pectoral muscles and then traveled in a thin, light brown trail down his torso almost like an arrow to the promised land below. Whoever put this man together certainly knew what they were doing because they gave him all the best parts.

"Your mother is just being stubborn," he argued playfully as he smacked my hip with his hand. "Let me up, I'll go get us something to clean up with before you leak on all the blankets."

It was my turn to laugh. "You just don't want me to leave the wet spot for you again."

"Damn right, woman. I fucked you to three orgasms, the least you could do is give up the dry side." He was teasing and we both knew it. Rich would take the wet spot every time, just to please me. I honestly thought he got off on making me the happiest woman in the world. Then again, since I only got to see him every other week, the other part of me thought maybe he was just always making up for lost time.

I wondered what things would be like for us if we lived in the same town and not nearly 600 miles apart. Leave it to me to find the one workplace romance that is perfect except for the fact that the man doesn't actually work in my office branch. He was on temporary, part-time loan to us for a specific campaign we were launching. Rich had family ties to the company we were representing, which is why they brought him in. He knew the inner workings and had an inside scoop on what the head honchos would be looking for in the rebranding we were pitching.

Every other week for the past three months, he came to stay and work. Before that, he was only here one week a month. Things were winding down soon with the campaign. Our client would be coming in, a month from now, for the final proposals and I knew they would be blown away. The problem was, once we clinched them and had contracts signed, Rich would no longer have to come work out of our office. He would be able to do his part remotely from where he lived. It scared me to think that I might lose him in the shuffle.

He asked me to transfer to his office, but I honestly couldn't do that. My mother had a stroke two years ago. Her declining health was what brought me back home to begin with. We were all the family each other had now. My mother had never left my hometown. Not once, in all the years of her life, had she ventured out of the county. It was insane to most people, but to her, it was just the way it was. She said she didn't need to go anywhere else.

That need not to go anywhere extended to my university graduation as well. I knew if she wouldn't show up to that, there was no way I would get her to agree to move 600 miles away. Her house was paid for, her final resting place was picked out and paid for, too. My mother was a planner. She would lie next to my father in the end.

She had been with him for thirty-six years when he passed,

and Mom never took another lover and rarely even spoke to men if she could help it. Her vows remained sacred to her even though my father was no longer of this world. I even attempted to convince her that the vows themselves say 'until death do us part'. She wouldn't speak to me for two weeks after that. She saw it as a betrayal of my father, and even in death, she defended his honor and kept her word. I admired it in a way, but then again, I also knew she was lonely. That was why I couldn't move away from her.

My mother needed someone to look after her now. Her left side was weak and according to her doctor she would never regain full function and strength again.

"What has your wheel spinning over there?"

I gave a startled little squeak as Rich settled down beside me and wiped up the mess he'd left between my legs. "Just thinking about possibilities."

His eyes twinkled as they met mine. "Really?"

Damn it. I didn't mean to get his hopes up. My sigh was enough to make his shoulders sag as the bright gleam of his eyes quickly dimmed. "Sorry, I was just thinking about my mom."

"You know, you could always try to get her to agree to one of those retirement communities where they still have independence, but there is a staff to help care for them."

My jaw dropped. I was appalled that he would suggest dropping my mother off at a facility to become someone else's problem. This was the one and only point of contention in our relationship. Outside of the two of us, he didn't seem to care about anything or anyone else. It always drove me so crazy – especially when one of those people he chose not to give a shit about was my mother – my only living relative.

"I still don't understand why you can't put in for a transfer here," I argued. It was something he wouldn't give me a real answer to. His grunt was another of his non-answers. "It's not like you have anyone back home to worry about. You've said it yourself, that's why you don't have any issue traveling back and forth as much as you do."

I glanced over at the frown on his face and watched as something played behind those soulful, whiskey-hued eyes of his. "It's not that easy for me, considering my position. Jobs here are easily filled. Back home, that office would be lost without me."

"Way to check your ego," I mumbled. He still heard and turned to his side so that he faced me instead of the ceiling.

"You know it's true. No one wants to pack up and go live in a small town to take on the little fish accounts when they can be here swimming in an ocean of whales."

"And sharks," I reminded him. There were a couple highly competitive individuals in my office who would just as soon steal a person's work as come up with something original on their own. I was lucky that I did a lot of pro-bono work for charities and had developed a signature style. It was hard to copy my designs and concepts since there were so many examples of it out there to compare to. It also helped that my bosses were normally on my side in the few instances where something came up. The fact was, I brought good publicity to the business. It helped when determining who to trust. That was another reason I couldn't transfer. I didn't think my bosses would let me go that easily.

"I'm not concerned with the sharks, my little goddess."

"Can you be concerned with what we're going to do once you're no longer needed in my office after this campaign launches?"

Rich sighed so heavily that I could feel the frustration coming off him in waves as he finally released the overlong breath. "I guess I could keep traveling back and forth, but the company won't want to keep paying those expenses." His eyes moved to meet my own. "We could be running the office where I live, babe. We would be the top dogs there and we'd be together. That means we would make our own schedules and be able to hire the people who work for us, so that we know they're team players."

His toothy grin was meant to enamor me, but instead, it just made me feel sad.

"I can't. I came here to take care of my mother, Rich. I don't know why you can't understand that. My mom is all I have in this world."

"You have me as well." His indignant huff after that ruffled my feathers, but I remained silent, so he continued. "Don't I matter at all? It's all about your mom, but if we don't figure this out, we'll be doomed to keep seeing each other only one week a month, two if we're lucky."

I continued to lie there quietly knowing that it would do no good to disagree. There was no use pointing out that he wasn't taking my professional position into account at all, and with the personal – he simply didn't even think my mother warranted such staunch loyalty from me. That was truly the one flaw Rich had that bothered me and made me wonder how important I really was to him. He didn't have family holding him back from a move. His only excuse was that he enjoyed being the biggest fish in a smaller pond. His ego wasn't more important than spending what time I had left with my mother. I couldn't seem to get him to understand that.

The past five months had been amazing with Rich. We started out with some harmless flirting when we were first thrown together on this job and from there it turned into a beautiful love affair. I didn't know how in the hell I would give him up. It was looking like I might have to though, and it killed me inside to know that neither of us was willing to sacrifice our places in this world for the other. It was impossible for me because of my mother, and I couldn't understand what was holding him back.

"Let's not fight. Do I get some closet space with this key of yours?" He finally asked before leaning over and nipping lightly at my overly sensitive nipple.

"Ouch! You jerk," I yelped before nodding my head. "Of course, you get a drawer, too, I might even make space for your toothbrush." I winked and grinned as he leaned in closer and used his lips to wipe the grin off my face. He sucked my bottom lip into his mouth and then nipped at it before releasing and planting a cute little kiss on the tip of my nose.

"My beautiful goddess always knows how to take care of her man."

I did. I would continue doing it too, as long as we were able. It was the future that worried me, especially since once again, he had finished inside me without protection. I couldn't take birth control because of the reactions I had to most of it. He knew that. Sometimes, I wondered if he was trying to get me pregnant, so that I would finally be convinced to move in with him. Rich explained before that he'd inherited a four-bedroom house from his family when they passed. Them being gone already was also the reason he had nothing holding him back from a move as opposed to my family situation. I had yet to see his house because the timing hadn't worked out, which was another issue for me. How was I supposed to just pick up and move to a town I'd never even stepped foot in?

I had planned to surprise him one weekend, and just show up, but before I could, he sent a text saying he had to go out of town to help a buddy of his move after his wife kicked him out. I was so thankful I got that text from him. It would have been awful to travel 600 miles and find him gone, then have to travel 600 more to get back home while swimming in disappointment. Between the two of our schedules, there just hadn't been an opportunity since then.

There were still so many doubts turning over in my mind about the move that would eventually need to be made. What if I hated his town, his house, or the job there? What if I did get pregnant before then? Would he give up all his worries to come be a family with us here? For every question that battered my heart, there seemed to be no answer in sight.

Rich had to go back soon, and I didn't want him going home

feeling like we weren't in a good place. I was woman enough to know that I was a bit jealous of his time at home. My insecurity reared its ugly head just enough to not want to push him into a bad spot before sending him back to an unfamiliar town. There were bound to be women there who would pick up where I left off in a heartbeat. Rich was a good-looking man, had a great job, and he was a monster in the sack. Yeah, I'm not too proud to admit that there's no way I'd send him home wanting for another week.

Instead, I did what any woman would do, and I wrapped him up in my body for another round of love making without all the serious talk hanging over our heads. Our problems would still be there to worry over later.

Chapter 2

March

Are you sure we really need to go out tonight? I kind of wanted to stay in and just be with you." I turned to look at Rich, who insisted on driving us to the restaurant. He had been complaining like this since we left, and it was starting to make me angry.

"All we ever do is stay in when you're here. I feel like the only places I've ever actually seen you are at work and at my place."

"You know why." His clipped tone hit my last nerve again. He continued to ping the damn thing until all I wanted to do was yank the steering wheel from his hands, crash us into the guardrail, and have it out with him in a good, old fashion screaming match. He had been doing his level best to ruin the night since I told him we had plans. My surprise for his birthday was about to be flushed down the toilet, and all because he didn't want to leave the house again.

"I understand that we don't get a lot of time together, but we haven't been out on a proper date since we first started dating. Maybe, I just want to go out once in a while and show off my hunky boyfriend."

I didn't miss the slight cringe before he covered it up and glanced my way with a too-wide smile that never reached his eyes. "Fine, but did we really need to spend more time with people from work?"

"Come on, you love Bridgette and Cliff. Stop being a grump and let's have a wonderful night."

After we got to the restaurant, Rich's phone started ringing. He took a quick glimpse and smiled. "Why don't you go on in and I'll be there in a few minutes. I have to take this."

"I can wait," I offered.

He quickly shook his head. "Go ahead. Order me a Gin and Tonic and I'll be along shortly." His smile turned glacial when his cell stopped ringing in his hands. I heaved out a sigh and then left the car to go meet Bridge and Cliff inside. They had texted just before we pulled up that they already had a seat in the quiet section near the back bar. I bypassed the hostess station and marched straight back, wondering – and not for the first time – if Rich had started seeing another woman back home, since it was clear that I didn't want to give up my life to transfer there.

My heart skipped a beat at the thought. Our relationship was still less than a year old, but that didn't matter. I'd given the man my heart months ago.

"Hey, Avi! You look beautiful tonight." Cliff stood and greeted me with a kiss on my cheek.

"Thank you," I returned while giving him a quick side hug.

"You really do look amazing in that dress." It was a black slip dress that hugged my breasts and draped like a waterfall of silk down to mid-thigh. I paired it with a white gold chain that held an orchid charm. Each petal of the orchid's flower was an Amethyst with two emeralds hugging it to represent the leaves of the plant. It had been a gorgeous birthday present from Rich last month and one I cherished. That reminded me.

"Did you bring it?"

"Of course, I brought it." Bridgette reached into her overly large handbag and pulled out the wrapped gift I had slipped her while we were at work yesterday. I knew there would be no way to conceal the gift with what I planned to wear tonight. I smoothed my dress down and took a seat while placing the gift in the chair next to mine where Rich would be sitting whenever he decided our date night was more important than his phone call.

We had to tell the waitress one more time to give us a few minutes when Rich still hadn't shown up. "Do you want me to go check on him?" Cliff finally asked.

"I think maybe you better. He didn't know I was bringing him out tonight for a birthday celebration. He was a little reluctant to come because going out means sharing our time with others." Cliff only nodded and stood to leave the table as Bridgette reached over and took my hand.

"Are you okay?" She asked, keeping her voice low.

"Please, don't ask me that. I don't want to become a blubbering mess here at the table."

"Aw, sweetie, I know the two of you are strained because of the whole, 'who should transfer thing' but it will be all right. It's so obvious that the man loves you. He can never take his eyes off of you at work."

"I think maybe he's seeing someone else," I admitted quickly before I could stop the words from falling out of my mouth.

"What? No way! That man adores you! He asked you to move in with him for God's sake."

"I know, but I turned him down because my mom is here, and I don't think it would be a smart move for my career. What if he's fed up with the fact that I won't sacrifice those things for him?"

"Why should it be you who sacrifices?" She asked.

"I don't know. He won't budge on the subject though, even

knowing my situation. I think maybe he's started seeing someone there. Lately, he gets more phone calls and texts that he has to answer, and I know they're not work related."

"Try not to jump to conclusions, sweetie. I'm sure it's nothing."

A simple nod of my head was the only answer I had for her. What else could I say? The man I loved had been pulling away over the past few weeks. I felt it. That coupled with the influx of calls and texts worried me.

A few minutes later, Rich and Cliff turned back up. Cliff had lost his usual jovial demeanor and Rich seemed ready to bolt. He barely sat in his seat, ignoring the package there, and then leaned in to offer a quick peck against my cheek before he stood up again. "Sorry, something came up back at home. I'm going to have to leave tonight to get back and handle it."

"What could have possibly come up on a Friday night?" I asked. I didn't maintain my focus on my boyfriend though, instead, my eyes drifted to Cliff who was unusually fidgety in his seat and throwing weird looks to Bridge.

"Why do you have to question everything?" Rich snapped which forced my attention back to him. I slid my chair back and stood.

"Do you think you can give me a ride home?" I asked Bridgette and Cliff.

"Sure, no problem," Bridgette said as she too stood, ready to leave.

"Jesus!" Rich huffed. "I'm sorry. Sit. Stay. Eat. I can't..." He seemed so flustered that I wasn't sure how to take what was happening. "I have to go pack and leave. Stay, have the dinner you planned. I'll call when I get in."

Rich left no room to argue as he turned and took off for the front of the restaurant leaving me standing there gawking after him. I glanced back down at the table after he was no longer in view and noticed that he left behind the gift I had waiting for him. As embarrassing as it was, there was no holding back the tears that fell.

"I don't even know what just happened." The shock in Bridgette's tone only caused a sob to break free. "I'm so sorry, come on, let's get you out of here, Avi."

My friend helped me outside as her man settled the bill for our drinks before meeting us at the car. I could tell by the look on his face, when he attempted to silently communicate with Bridgette, that he knew exactly what was going on with Rich, but also that he wouldn't tell me.

"He didn't even take the gift I got him," I complained through my tears as I held the box in my lap on the way back to my place. The wrapping paper had been ripped when Rich sat on it for that brief moment in time before bailing on his own surprise birthday dinner.

"It's probably for the best."

"Cliff!" Bridgette's shocked gasp stunned me for a moment before his words sank in.

This had been the end of us. The end of me and Rich and I didn't know why or understand any of it. It took a while of being lost in my own pity party to realize that Cliff hadn't taken me straight home.

"What are we doing over here?" I finally asked him when I glanced up and realized that we were nowhere near my place. The guilty eyes that met mine in the rearview mirror told me everything I needed to know. "You're giving him time to clear out his things, aren't you?"

"Avi," he started to say, the sad tone of his voice doing nothing but grating on my already frayed nerves. The tears fell hot and fast down my face once again.

"I don't understand." The words were whispered from my lips, but Cliff spoke in response anyway.

"Sometimes, it's nothing for you to understand. Just remember that this isn't on you – not at all. It's on him."

"Then why are you helping him?" I argued, my voice sounding strained with the emotions I'd been going through.

"Believe it or not, I'm not helping him, Avi. I'm helping you."

"That's not what this feels like."

"Going back, while he's there clearing out his shit, is not what you need to see right now."

"He's really doing it?" I questioned, even though I already knew the truth. Only a curt nod answered my question. "I don't understand why."

"I don't think you want to know."

His response startled me and when our eyes met, there was a deeper sadness that settled in his. He knew more than he was willing to tell. My mind went back to my earlier conversation with Bridgette, when I confided in her that I thought the man I loved had started seeing someone else. My stomach clenched and then rolled.

"Pull over!" The demand was swift and urgent enough that Cliff didn't mess around, he pulled over just in time for me to throw the door open and heave out the little bit of liquid that had been on my stomach. I never wanted to be one of those women who fell apart over a man. I swore to myself that it would never happen to me. For that reason, it stung that much more when I found myself puking into the gutter because my emotions were in such turmoil. Sadly, it felt like the only way to purge some of the pain.

When I finally managed to pull myself together, Cliff handed back a napkin to wipe my mouth with. "It'll get better, Avi."

"Why is he doing this?"

"He's a selfish bastard." His response was swift and angry, but he didn't offer any further details. I couldn't fault Cliff for not breaking whatever confidence he had with Rich. It wasn't his place and I felt bad pushing for information because no one wanted to be put in the position of being the man in the middle of a couple as they split up. I respected that, even though I wanted to do whatever was necessary to get the man to fess up. It wasn't really his place, though. It had been Rich's place to tell me what was going on in our own relationship and instead, he chose the coward's way out.

$$\mathcal{L}$$

I refused to let Bridgette or Cliff come into my place with me when they finally took me back home. Instead, I walked in, locked the door behind me, and then took a deep breath to fortify myself for what I would see. The one thing that I didn't see was the key to my place left behind anywhere. He had apparently taken that with him. I didn't know why, and frankly was pissed about it, because that meant I would have to change the locks. There was no way he was keeping a key to my place after the way he had just treated me.

"I didn't even get to tell him happy birthday," I said out loud to the empty room as I threw the gift I had gotten for his birthday onto the table. The extra pair of running shoes he brought to keep here were gone, no longer lying beside the front door. I locked up and took the time to change the alarm code on the panel. Even if he did use his key again before I changed the locks, it would trip the alarm that he would no longer be able to turn off.

It would serve him right to have to deal with the police after leaving me at the restaurant. I moved to my bedroom and noticed immediately that the closet door was left ajar. His side of the closet had been cleared out – not that there had been much in there. He had hung two suits, a pair of jeans, and a casual sweater. In the drawer by the window, there used to be a few t-shirts, socks, and boxer briefs. The drawer stood empty when I pulled it open. All of his hygiene items had been left behind in my bathroom, as if he forgot to check in there before he took off.

I went back out to the kitchen, grabbed the trash can, and

made my way back to scoop all of his man-scented products into the garbage. His toothbrush and comb joined the rest. Just like that, there was no trace of him anywhere in my home. At least, I thought I had purged the last of it. It wasn't until I laid down on the bed and the scent of him wafted up around me that I realized there was still a little bit of him left. He'd been staying here all week, so the sheets carried his scent and helped to scar his memory on my heart.

With the last dregs of my energy, I stripped the bed, threw an extra blanket down on the bare mattress, and then climbed under the quilt I kept in my chair. I'd make the bed tomorrow after I washed everything.

ALSO BY ANNE STORM

The Groupie Journal

Letters to Lily

His Bittersweet Regret

Bad at Love

TFO

The Fortunate Ones

Robeson Family Novels (standalones)

The Forgotten Wife

When the Last Petal Falls

Mirage Island Mates

Into the Grasslands

Beyond the Grasslands

Standalone Shifter Novel

Winter Wolves

The Ancients Series

Shadows of the Ancients

Falling into the White

Branches of the Willow

Bound by the Moon

Vukodlak Brew Series

Entwined

Enraged

The Awakening Series

Birthrights

Revelations

Incarnations

Death Viewers

Breathless

ABOUT THE AUTHOR

Christine Michelle also write's under the name Anne Storm.
Anne Storm's books:
Dark romance/subjects with major triggers
Christine Michelle's books:
(mild) MC Romance, Rock Star Romance, and other
Contemporary Romance
Paranormal Fantasy & Romance

If you want to learn more about Christine, her books, or her crazy adventures into the wilderness, you can find out more through the following links:
Website & Newsletter sign up:
www.moonlitdreams.org
Signing up for the newsletter also gets you first option at future Beta reading and ARC (advanced reader copy) giveaway opportunities!
**Universal links to everything
(social media, book links, and more)**
https://linktr.ee/christinemichelle

- facebook.com/M00nlitDreams
- instagram.com/christinemichelle_annestorm
- tiktok.com/@christine.michelle.books
- bsky.app/profile/annestorm.bsky.social